D1267629

Dear McKinnon

DANIELLE KEIL

Dear McKinnon
Love Notes Series

Copyright © 2022 by Danielle Keil

Cover design and interior formatting by
Stephanie Anderson, Alt 19 Creative

ALSO BY
Danielle Keil

The Parkdale Series

The Pact Series

The Ainsworth Royals:
The Next Gen Series

Love Notes Series

To everyone who remembers their high school years fondly. And if you don't, feel free to live inside the world of Ryder High instead. They'll welcome you with open arms and make it better.

"Are you excited?" Skye exclaimed, her voice jumping an octave. She almost squeaked when she was passionate, like a mouse.

It was probably the reason most people *called* her Mouse. It didn't make sense to me until a few weeks ago, when she got over enthusiastic about Jeremy asking her to the Valentine's Day Dance. She squeaked for a full day and a half after that.

"For what?" I asked, turning back to my locker and searching for my algebra textbook. I remembered putting it there yesterday, but that didn't mean much. I wasn't a slob by any means, but organization wasn't my strongest skill.

Skye leaned against the row of metal lockers next to mine, staring up at the ceiling as if it were full of glittering stars, or big, fluffy clouds. Her head was always up there anyway; reality was hard for Skye to wrap her brain around and she lived in her oblivion most days.

"The new secret admirer, of course," Skye muttered, her hands clutched to her chest. Her pink skater dress hung to her thighs, thick, wooly white tights covering her legs and ending in a pair of ankle boots.

She was always more fashionable than me, but definitely in the winter. Cold weather called for jeans and a hoodie, maybe with a t-shirt underneath if it was especially chilly.

I paused and looked around my locker door at her, pushing up my ever-slipping glasses. "Excuse me?"

Skye rolled her eyes. "McKinnon, you have to have heard about the secret admirers by now!"

My lips stayed shut as I blinked what I could only assume was Morse code for "hell no". Not only did the term 'secret admirer' sound outdated and off-putting, but we were in high school, not second grade. What seventeen-year-old got excited for a secret admirer?

Skye's mouth, and hands, dropped. "Are you serious? You've been here almost two months and you don't know about the monthly secret admirers?"

Finally, I found my textbook, shoved it into my backpack and slammed my locker shut. "If I knew, do you think I would be having this insane conversation with you right now?"

Lifting my long, blonde hair from under straps, careful not to damage the curls I spent half an hour on this morning, I started down the hallway, knowing Skye would follow.

We met the first day I came to Ryder High, right after winter break. Moving to a new town, and a new state, over break was hard. Starting a new school right away was even harder, especially half way through junior year.

Skye took me under her wing the very first time she set eyes on me. She was like that; a one-woman welcoming committee. While she wasn't labeled the most popular girl in school, everyone knew her. They all had some sort of story to tell with her. She flitted about group to group, making sure everyone was taken care of like a mother hen. I had yet to meet someone who had anything bad to say about her.

It was overwhelming at first, the attention she gave me, but after a while, I got used to it. There was so much I didn't know about Ryder High, it was nice to have someone on my side. Coming from being homeschooled, there was a lot about public high school I didn't know at *all*, and appreciated having Skye make sure I didn't make too much of a fool of myself.

The stomp of her boots echoed down the hall as she jogged behind me. "The secret admirers. Every month, a junior or senior boy puts a note in the locker of a girl. Or a boy. Honestly, they're rather inclusive these days. Quite refreshing."

Monthly? Parts of high school really confused me, but this I was not expecting.

I scrunched my brow. "And?" I prompted, waiting for her to get to the actual point. I was a straight forward type of girl, and Skye lived for tangents.

"Today is March first, McKinnon. That means someone is going to get a note in their locker *today*. Oh!" Her blue eyes grew wide. "Maybe they already have! I wonder who it is. Last month, it was a senior named

Tabitha. Do you know Tabitha? She's on the field hockey team."

I shook my head. I barely knew anyone other than Skye. Some other girls in my classes were friendly, but it didn't extend much past the classroom. I enjoyed keeping to myself, as it gave me a chance to watch my surroundings and figure people out. People watching was an excellent hobby, especially for an avid reader like me.

One thing I did while people watching was assign random strangers to characters in the books I read. Sometimes I would cast an entire novel in a lunch period. Sometimes it took a few days to collect them all. And sometimes I skipped around, picking characters from different books based on who I saw.

"Well, Jamison was her secret admirer, and it was just *so romantic*. He left all these adorable clues, and each one had a flower taped to it. By the end, she had an entire bouquet."

Sighing, I turned the corner, heading toward Algebra. Skye's first class was only a few halls away, and knowing her, she would sprint to be on time just so she could finish her story.

"I don't know Tabitha. Or Jamison. But what's the point? A girl gets a note from a guy and then what?"

Part of me was curious. If this was a monthly thing, how did the boys choose? How did it end up being *one* guy each month? Was there a sign-up sheet? A Google Doc? Did someone use a randomizer website with everyone's names thrown in and assign them a month? What if the person they chose to pursue was taken when their turn came up?

There were so many variables, it made my head spin. None of it made sense, but none of it mattered to me anyway. I wasn't going to be chosen. I was the new girl; guys didn't even know me yet.

"So, they get the note that starts it off. Like an invitation of sorts. They can accept or deny. After that, they have one month to figure out who the guy is. He can leave his clues in any way he wants. Some just do flat out notes taped to the locker with a stat on them or something. But a lot of them get creative and make it a fun game."

"And if you don't figure it out by the end of the month?"

Skye paused outside my classroom, tapping her perfectly manicured nail against her pale pink lips. "Hmm. I'm not sure that's happened yet? I mean, naturally everyone is in on it and helps figure it out. There are rules—"

"Naturally," I interjected with a hint of sarcasm.

"But," Skye continued, glaring at me, "any bit of help helps. The longest the mystery has taken was three weeks, I think? Oh, and guess what?"

"There's more?" I deadpanned. I glanced inside, hoping no one was sitting in my usual seat. I liked to sit in the back corner, where I could see out the sliver of a window in the door and the windows along the side that looked over the garden the Home Ec classes used to grow fruits and veggies.

"Of course there's more, silly. This isn't some thrown together crazy game. It's intricate and planned and has been going on for *years* here at Ryder."

"Years? Then how have—" The sound of the bell interrupted me. It was time for Skye to split.

She headed down the hall backwards. "I'll tell you more at lunch!" she shouted, adding a wave before she turned and sprinted to her class, her brown bob bouncing around her shoulders.

I opened the door, holding it for my teacher behind me.

"As long as you're in before I am, you aren't marked tardy, Miss McKinnon," she said with a smile.

"Appreciated, Mrs. Saletta," I replied. I took my seat and looked out over the garden, thinking about what Skye said.

A million questions ran through my mind. The entire operation made no sense, yet Skye made it seem like a big deal. There were only so many months out of the year that the boys could even do this game. Which meant only a sliver of the female population would get chosen. Well, unless they did it in the summer too, but...

I shook my head, not wanting to think about it anymore. The more I thought, the more nothing made sense. Why would people get so excited over a secret admirer? How many girls cried themselves to sleep on the first of each month when they realized they weren't chosen? Were friendships ruined because of this? And what more did Skye have to tell me?

Mrs. Saletta cleared her throat, getting our attention. I forced myself to stop thinking about it and focus on algebra. Math was one of my worst subjects, and I needed all the attention I could give it.

Besides, I was the new girl. There was no way I would ever be chosen, and I would be of no help to whoever was. Therefore, the whole secret admirer situation shouldn't interest me at all.

Chapter 2

M y pulse stopped. Really, I think my heart skipped a few beats before flatlining.

What. Is. That?

A tealish-blue colored envelope rested on top of my stack of textbooks on the bottom of my locker.

Like someone had shoved it through the vents at the top.

My name was written on the outside, in cursive, in ink. Teal ink. Darker than the envelope, but purposefully chosen.

I didn't want to touch it. Everything Skye said earlier this morning ran through my mind.

One girl. One girl gets a letter on the first of the month.

Today was March first. This was a letter.

Well, I didn't *know* that for sure. Technically, it was an envelope. I had to open it to assess what was inside.

But all my mind could think of was that it was a letter. From a secret admirer.

I broke out into a nervous sweat, my palms clammy at my sides as I stared into my locker. Blinking was the only thing my brain allowed me to do at the moment besides stare.

"Stop being foolish, Macks. You are not the chosen one. That's main character energy, and you are a sidekick. You're not even a sidekick, you're a tertiary character. Background actor. Extra. That's it— you're an extra in this movie of high school craziness," I muttered to myself.

Dropping my backpack next to my locker, I bent down and picked up the envelope. Whoever left it obviously was mistaken.

But they did write my name in the most gorgeous calligraphy. The loops on the M and the K were exquisite and the shading...

"Gah! Just open it!" I whispered.

"Open what?" Skye's voice said next to me.

I jumped a foot into the air, almost smashing my head on the shelf. Standing and spinning around, I shoved my hands behind my back, keeping them inside the locker while I looked at Skye.

"What are you hiding?" she asked suspiciously. Her eyes narrowed as if she was trying to x-ray through my body and see what was behind me.

"No-no-nothing," I stammered, unable to keep the blush from rising on my cheeks. I was a terrible liar, especially when my face couldn't hide emotions.

"Hand it over, girlfriend."

I shook my head, blonde curls flying everywhere. "I can't."

"Why not?"

"I... I..." I had no good answer, but something told me I couldn't let Skye see the envelope. That possibly held a letter. That potentially had an invitation or secret admirer clue on it.

Skye paused, her hand still waiting palm up in front of my face.

If I didn't show it to her, then I could hide it. I could pretend that it didn't exist and I wasn't part of this weird game the entire school went crazy over. I could rip the letter to shreds and ignore it for the rest of eternity.

Maybe everyone would assume no one was chosen for March. Or that whoever they chose wanted to remain in secret. Surely that had happened before... right?

"Ahem. While we're still young and beautiful, darling."

My heart pounded so loud I thought the whole building could hear it. My face was on fire and my vision blurred.

In the end, I gave in. I didn't know what else to do. Slipping my hand from behind my back, I showed Skye the tip of the teal envelope.

Her eyes grew wide. Her hands flew to her face. And before I knew it, Mouse returned.

"Oh my God, oh my God, oh my GOD, McKinnon!! You were chosen!! You're the girl of the month!" she shrieked at the top of her lungs.

I lunged at her, slapping my hand over her mouth and pulling her in tight like a hug. It wasn't a hug, though, it was a restraint position as I tried to keep her excitement level at a two instead of a ten. I kept her close for a good five seconds before letting her go.

"Can you keep it down? I don't need the whole school hearing you!" I said through gritted teeth. A quick glance showed that only a few people paused and looked our way. More than likely, everyone was used to a Skye outburst, and it didn't faze them anymore.

But to me, it was a blinking neon sign with a giant arrow pointing right at me.

"Don't want anyone hearing? McKinnon, this is *huge*. Huger than huge. The hugest!" Mouse shrieked, but thankfully in a more hushed tone.

I bit my lip, still holding the envelope behind my back. My sweaty palm creased it already, probably smearing the ink all over. My hand would end up looking like a Smurf soon.

"I don't even know what it is..."

"Then *open* it. But I can tell you, it's a letter. It's *the* letter. You're in!"

I was in. The chosen one. But did I *want* to be? I didn't know any of the guys here at Ryder High. I stayed far away because, honestly, they scared me. They were always yelling, throwing things, being loud and rowdy. It was easier to mind my own business and stay out of the ruckus.

So, if I *was* chosen, which I still didn't know because I hadn't opened the damn letter yet, then how the hell would I be able to figure out who it was?

"Are you going to open it or what? I'm not below tickling you to get it out of your hands," Skye said, snapping me out of my thoughts.

Thankfully, it was lunch period, and we didn't have to rush off. Instead, I could spend the required amount of time analyzing every detail and determine exactly what I was dealing with.

"McKinnon!"

"Okay, okay!" Turning into my locker, I shielded the paper with my body, but allowed Skye to squeeze in next to me. Her signature orchid perfume wafted through my nose, the sweet floral scent calming my racing heart.

"Go any slower and you'll miss your end of month deadline, girlfriend."

I sucked in a breath, checked Skye with my shoulder, and slid my finger under the flap.

The paper on the inside was a gorgeous shade of lavender, matching the inner lining of the envelope. It was all intricately planned, just as Skye mentioned earlier.

I had no idea what I was getting myself into.

Chapter 3

McKinnon–

The men of Ryder High invite you to become part of an exclusive club of exquisite people like yourself. Ones who are admired and revered, but from afar.

Acceptance of this invitation will start your month-long journey into finding out who sent you this letter. The man who craves your attention, yet strays from your spotlight. He may be someone you know, or someone you have never met.

But he knows you. And he chose you. In the end, it is his wish to be with you in whatever context you prefer. It's all up to you. Nothing during this month is mandatory. You can stop at any time. If you are ever uncomfortable, a neutral party can be spoken with, and alternatives can be made.

<u>You are in control.</u>

The secret admirers are chosen and vetted. There is no mal-intent involved with this invitation. You may choose to decline the invitation all together without any backlash. You have our guarantee that no harm will come to you in any form.

If you wish for more information regarding the history of the secret admirers, please text the number at the bottom. All your questions, within reason and without ruining the mystery, will be answered to the best of our ability.

For now, the first question is for you.

Do you accept?

Sincerely—
Your Secret Admirer

turned the letter over in my hands, trying to see if there was more. But that was it. I had to admit, they covered their bases and made it sound tempting. They also made the whole thing feel...comfortable?

"I. Can't. Believe. It!" Skye squealed again, right in my ear.

I backed up, shoving the letter under a textbook before moving away from her for some air.

It was me. I was the chosen one for the month. And I was in complete control over what happened.

The letter said I could back out right now, and no one would be the wiser. Considering how carefully the letter was worded, it seemed like whoever ran this had the power to make sure no one would know.

But ... the letter also made it sound fun. An exclusive club of people. It was somewhere I could finally fit in.

"What do I need to know?" I asked Skye with the most determination and confidence I could muster.

She threw my backpack at me, slammed my locker shut, and looped her arm through mine. "*Everything.*"

I sighed. Was I getting in over my head? The spotlight would be on me all month as I figured out clues, hopefully with the help of people I could trust. Right now, that circle included Skye, and that was about it. Maybe I would make more friends out of this.

Would people try to screw me over? Would they give me bad advice or lead me on wild goose chases? What if someone figured out who the secret admirer was before I did and tried to keep me away from him?

"Skye, this is so ... much," I said, waving my hands in the air, unable to come up with the exact word I was looking for. "What am I even doing?" I lamented.

A huge grin broke across her face. "Don't worry. I have you covered. If you want to do it, that is."

"How many people have ever turned it down?"

She paused, thinking. "Since I've known about it? One or two, maybe. There was one girl who stopped playing halfway through, but she was going through a lot of other things at the time."

I frowned. "What happened to her?"

Skye's grin turned into a sad smile. "It ended up being cute, actually. She called the neutral party, and they called the whole thing off at that exact moment. But two days later, the guy outed himself to her, and they ended up getting together. Her mother had been diagnosed with cancer during the month, and he was there for her the entire time. Her mom recovered, and last I heard, they were still together now in college."

We pushed through the doors to the cafeteria and headed toward the long line. It took us so long to go over the letter, we only had half the lunch period left.

"Okay ... so, if I accept, what else? Wait, *how* do I accept? It didn't say."

Skye grabbed us both cheeseburgers and a bag of chips before answering. "You do nothing. If you accept, another note will be on your locker tomorrow and your game officially begins. If you want out, text the number. If you have questions, ask me, and if I can't answer, text the number."

We wove our way through the crowded tables before finding an empty one. I looked around nervously, trying to see if any boy was watching me. Would it be someone in this cafeteria? A guy in my classes?

Suddenly, it felt like the entire school shrunk, closing in around me.

"Why me?" I finally asked.

Skye scanned me from top to bottom with a serious look on her face. "Why *not* you? You're hot. You're smart. You're new, which means interesting to a number of people right off the bat. Plus, think of it this way. Someone noticed you. He had to have noticed you right away for them to choose you this month. These things are planned, like I said. Whoever the guy is chose you at least a few weeks ago."

All the blood drained from my face at that comment. "A few *weeks* ago? Someone here has had me on their radar and I've had no idea? That's.... terrifying."

A shiver traveled down my spine. While Skye sat in front of me, scarfing down her cheeseburger and chips like nothing was the matter, I couldn't eat. My stomach was in knots. I didn't like being watched. People watching was *my* hobby, but knowing someone had been full on keeping track of me was horrifying. Did I have a stalker? Or was this a prank?

"Are you going to accept?" Skye asked, covering her full mouth with her hand.

My brain flip-flopped between yes and no a million times. It was exciting. But it also was petrifying.

Everyone would know me, and fast. I wouldn't be able to hide in the shadows, at least for this month.

I was the chosen one.

But did I want to be?

I didn't tell a single person about the note for the rest of the day. I kept it shoved between textbooks at the bottom of my locker until it was time to leave. Then, I slid it between the pages of a random notebook and threw it into my backpack. I couldn't look at it. Every time I thought about it, I got goosebumps.

And I wasn't sure if they were the good or bad kind yet.

The entire bus ride home, I was a nervous wreck. Not that anyone noticed. I sat by myself in the middle of the bus, looking out the window the entire time with my backpack on my lap, my arms wrapped around it, keeping it safe and secure.

I heard the whispering in the halls after lunch. Apparently, it was customary for the receiver to get her letter early in the day, and no one had heard anything yet.

Rumors started to swirl that whoever got it had rejected the invitation, something no one had done yet this school year. Some other people started saying that whoever got the letter was going to stay in secret.

If they only knew.

I had so many questions running through my mind. Skye walked me through a bit of the nuances of the mystery and how to play along, but really, it was all still crazy to me.

What if I accepted? How would it change my everyday life? Would people hate me? Skye didn't say anything about the retaliation that came from being chosen, but there had to be a massive number of jealous girls out there each month.

Plus, there were logistical questions. Things the person on the other end of the number probably could answer. But would I look like a fool by asking? Obviously they knew I was new and would give me some grace, right?

How long had this tradition of sorts been going on? Why did everyone just accept it and not think that it was overly odd and stalkerish?

"Hey, isn't this your stop?" Someone poked me in the side, jolting me out of my deep thoughts. I glanced around, finding a kind smile upon a guy's face. I didn't know his name, but he always sat in the seat across the aisle from me. We had never spoken before.

I jumped to my feet, clutching my bag and sending him a quick thanks as I jogged down the aisle.

"Sorry!" I told the driver as I scrambled down the steps and onto the sidewalk.

I typed the code into the garage keypad and let myself in. There were no cars in the garage, meaning I was home alone. Mom would most likely be out running errands and Dad wouldn't be home until dinner.

Which gave me more time to think about this invitation.

I wanted to get answers. But I didn't want to look like an idiot.

Flopping onto my bed, I used one hand to dig into my backpack and find the envelope. It was slightly smooshed and wrinkled, the gorgeous ink a little smudged.

Flattening the letter between my hands, I read it over again, trying to find any nuance I could to convince myself *not* to accept.

When I changed from maybe to a yes, I didn't realize until just now. Now I was trying to talk myself *out* of it instead of into it.

Why shouldn't I accept? Someone was interested in me for the first time in my life. When Mom homeschooled me, I still joined some clubs and easy sports. But even there I was overlooked. I stayed in the corner, to myself, and got the job done. I didn't stick out.

So *where* did this mystery secret admirer find me? How did he see me? Why did he choose me?

I stared at the letter for so long, I lost track of time. Mom's hollers to come down for dinner brought me back to reality.

I had to stop obsessing over it. There needed to be a clear-cut answer somewhere. I just didn't know where.

Mom kept the conversation going throughout dinner, with me chiming in only bits and pieces about my day. We weren't the most talkative family, so no one noticed anything was off.

After cleaning up, I rushed back to my room to get my homework done. I kept the letter out of sight and out of mind while I focused on my work. I wouldn't let the invitation come between me and my grades, no matter what I chose.

The blaring of the alarm from my phone woke me. I bolted upright, the book resting in my hand getting tossed across my bed and tumbling to the floor.

It was morning. Time to get ready for school.

And that meant...by default, I had accepted.

I rushed to the bathroom to get ready. The letter said that I could opt out at any time. But Skye said that by not contacting anyone overnight, it was an automatic assumption of acceptance.

After throwing on a pair of jeans and a different hoodie, I rushed downstairs and swiped a fresh bagel off the counter before running out to meet the bus. I wasn't late, but moving faster made my brain not think about the consequences of my inaction.

"You accepted!" Skye's high-pitched squeal greeted me in the bus lobby. She must have been waiting for me, because the second I walked through the doors, I was attacked.

"Huh?" I questioned, jostling my backpack higher on my shoulder. I shivered, the cold breeze from the doors to the outside following me inside.

"You. Accepted!" she repeated, throwing her arms around me and squeezing me tight.

My face dropped. I quickly looked around, trying to see what was happening. Sure enough, eyes were on me from all around, some people attempting to be subtle with their points, some not.

"What's going on?" I asked Skye, pulling her out of the lobby as fast as I could and down the hall toward my locker.

"You accepted. What part about those two words are confusing? Am I not saying them clearly?" she questioned, a confused look on her face.

I shook my head. "No, nothing about those words are—ugh, forget it. Just...*how* did you know I accepted?"

A laugh escaped her lips. "Oh, that's easy. Because of that!"

I followed her outstretched finger pointing down the hall to my locker, where a teal blue envelope and a rose were taped. I believe I stopped breathing in that moment. It was different than when my heart stopped yesterday, but similar in the whole death is imminent feeling.

"What's that?" I whispered. My breathing resumed for me to push out words, but I still didn't feel any air in my lungs.

"That," Skye squeaked, "is your first clue." She bounced on her toes and clapped her hands like an excited toddler.

"And how many people have seen it?"

That made her pause. "I'm not sure? But probably enough for the school to realize there's a new player?"

"And how many people know it's me?"

I stood frozen in the same spot down the hall from my locker. I didn't go any closer, in case people didn't know it was mine yet.

Casting a side glance over to my friend, I found her pink nail tucked between her teeth, her brows knitted together.

"Umm..." she whispered. "Sorry?"

"What?"

Skye sighed and dropped her hands. "I may have gotten a tad bit over zealous. I mean, it's a new secret admirer, the start of a new month, and it's someone I know personally! It's going to be so much fun, McKinnon, just wait and see. We'll figure out who your secret admirer is in no time, and you'll get to know him, and the two of you will fall madly in—"

"What. Did. You. Do."

Her lips clamped shut mid- sentence. I watched as the little light bulb inside her brain finally clicked on.

"You ... didn't want anyone to know?"

I couldn't answer that. Because, by default, accepting the invitation meant everyone would know, eventually. This whole secret admirer thing seemed like a big deal to the student body, something I didn't quite understand. Yet.

Sucking in a deep breath, I held it for a moment before pursing my lips and letting it out slowly. "Not really. But I guess I can't hold it against you. I mean, there's a rose taped to my locker. Tons of people have probably seen it already."

A small, timid smile crossed Skye's lips, as if she were asking permission to be happy about the ordeal again. I gave her a half smile in acknowledgement, and her face lit up.

"Yes! She's in!"

I didn't open the envelope right away, much to Skye's dismay. The warning bell rung as we approached my locker, causing us all to scatter. Skye begged me to open it, but I had to be on the other side of the building in less than two minutes, and I had yet to switch out the items in my bag.

So, just like last night, I shoved it between the pages of a notebook and dumped it unceremoniously into my backpack. Someone behind me gasped as I did, causing me to turn around and check to see who was watching.

A girl with long brown hair stared at me as if I had committed a felony. Her eyes were wide, her hand over her mouth shaped in an "O".

I stared back at her in confusion before she realized, then bolted.

Here I was, barely in the game, and already ruffling feathers. I guess the letters should have been treated like gold instead of thrusted into a book, but honestly, I didn't have time to make that choice.

Sprinting to Algebra, I slipped in just before Mrs. Saletta came strolling down the hallway. We had a pop quiz today, which made me forget all about the new letter until lunch.

Skye met me at the entrance to the cafeteria, surrounded by a group of girls I didn't know all the names of. I tried to pay attention during class and catch some names here and there, just in case we were assigned a project, but not many stuck.

"There she is! The newest contender! Ladies, who do we have in the running for secret admirer this month?" Skye asked, spinning on the toe of her Chucks to walk into the cafeteria.

All the girls next to her did the same, leaving me baffled by the doors. As soon as they slammed shut, I came to and scrambled after them.

"Well, Henry is still free. He dumped Charlotte about four months ago, remember? And Josh hasn't been one of the guys yet this year," a girl with short red hair said while picking up a tray.

"Yeah, but rumor has it he's screwing Jade on the side. I doubt he would be on the short list if he's doing that," another girl answered. I think she was in my Spanish class, but had no idea what her name was.

"Ladies, ladies. Good answers only, please," Skye reprimanded, handing me a tray and pushing me through the crowd toward her. "Did you read the letter yet? I bet we can narrow down the list significantly from the first clue alone."

I bit my lip. "Um, no."

Gasps rose around me, causing my cheeks to flush.

"No, that's alright! If you don't mind, can we open it with you at the table?" Skye asked, noticing my nervousness and using her tone to chastise the girls at the same time. I nodded, and we remained quiet.

It didn't stop the rest of the cafeteria from gossiping, however. As we walked to our table, I caught snippets of conversations, clearly directed at me.

"Who is she anyway? I don't even remember ever seeing her here."

"Honestly, who would be interested in that? Does she own anything except jeans and hoodies?"

"I bet it's one of the nerds this month. No way would one of the popular guys be going for her."

I kept the quiver in my lips from showing until we got to the table, where I slunk down and tried to hide. I wanted to pull my hood over my head and tune out the entire room, but someone stopped me with a hand on my shoulder. Peeking up from under some of my hair, I found a girl with bright green eyes and naturally wavy brown hair that came just past her shoulders.

"I'm Spencer. And don't let them get to you. There's a whole slew of girls that will be super jealous they weren't picked. Most of us realize that there's only so many months in a year and we'll probably never be picked. Once you accept that, it's way more fun to play along. And if we are ever chosen, it'll be a great surprise. Keeping our hopes low helps everything in this situation. So, ignore them. They'll get over it."

I smiled at her and sat up straighter. "Thanks. I'm not used to being the center of attention. Like, at all. I'm an only child and I've been homeschooled until now."

Spencer laughed. "Don't worry. We have your back. And remember, if you ever want to bail, you totally can. People have done it before. You wouldn't be the first one."

I nodded and began to eat my lunch with a bit more confidence flowing through my veins. Even if I accidentally accepted, maybe it wouldn't be all bad.

"So? Are we reading the letter or what!" the blonde girl in front of me asked.

"Oh yeah. Sorry." I turned around and grabbed the envelope from my bag, placing it on the table between all of us.

The writing on the outside was the same as yesterday. I wondered if someone had taken the time to write it on a bunch, or made a new one every day.

"Ahem," Skye cleared her throat. "It's your envelope. You open it, silly!"

I chuckled nervously, grabbing for it while my cheeks flushed again.

Slicing the paper open, I pulled out the letter and unfolded it.

"Dear McKinnon," I started, scanning the note quickly for anything that jumped out at me, but finding nothing. I coughed and started over.

"McKinnon. Thank you for accepting your invitation. Honestly, I was a little worried you wouldn't. Being new, not knowing a lot of people, not knowing *me*, must be intimidating. This whole secret admirer thing probably sounds like a lot of craziness to you, but to us here at Ryder High, it's important. It allows couples who otherwise may never have met to fall in love. It allows a no-strings attached chance to get to know someone. You may have to figure out who I am, but I've already learned a lot about you. And not in a stalkerish way. Okay, I guess it all sounds stalkerish."

I paused, wanting to giggle, but also not wanting to offend the girls sitting around me. They all took this seriously, even if my secret admirer was agreeing with me on how creepy it kind of sounded.

"Okay, so what I'm hearing so far is it's someone who is nervous or talkative. Who fits that description?" Spencer questioned.

They all stayed silent, pondering.

"Too many," Skye responded. "Keep reading. We need more."

I took a swig of my water before continuing. So far, so good.

"Um, okay, stalkerish, stalkerish, right, here we go." It took a second to get back to the spot I left off, leaving everyone on the edge of their seats. I marked the sentence with my thumb and peeked at my audience, finding a few more girls had joined us, standing behind the girls I didn't know the names of across the table.

Gulping, I continued. "Anyway, I'm glad you accepted. I think this month is going to be a lot of fun. What I'm asking is for you to try a lot of this on your own. I don't imagine you know a ton of us guys here yet, so it will be hard. But together, I think we can manage. Your instinct will be to ask the girls surrounding you." I paused and looked up again, but instead of regarding the girls in front of me, I searched the cafeteria, as if he were watching me right now. I shook my head and let out a soft laugh, remembering that the note was attached to my locker early this morning. Obviously, he wasn't watching me *right now*.

"Your instinct will be to ask people surrounding you, but don't let them take control. My clues should help you narrow things down little by little, even if you don't know a lot of people here at Ryder. So, if you are reading this out loud, stop here. The rest is just for you. It's our first secret, meant just for you and me."

I stopped, folding the letter in half and shoving it back into the envelope as fast as I could. Multiple groans reached my ears, but I just smiled.

It was our first secret. Something meant just for him and I. It made me ... almost giddy inside. I didn't know why, but I felt like I already knew him, and that he understood me.

It had to be someone who had access to me. Tuning out the angry comments around me, I tried to think of how many guys I had multiple classes with.

It didn't work well, since I couldn't match too many faces to names, especially guys. I made a mental note to start jotting down names or at least descriptions of people in my classes.

But for now ... I wanted to read the rest of the note. And it had to be in private.

"Gotta go," I announced to the upset group around me. In the last few minutes, the crowd had grown. Word must have spread that I was the girl of the month, and with me reading the note out loud like a fool, it drew a good number of onlookers.

But the rest wasn't for them. It was for me. I slipped my backpack over my shoulder, grabbed my tray, and headed toward the trash cans.

The doors clanged as I pushed through them while trying to think of where I could go to read the rest. I didn't have much time left in the period, nor did I know of too many personal places.

In the end, the student union was the answer, even if it was full of people. But considering I left the envelope on the lunch table, it would look as if I were just reading a regular letter.

Even better, as soon as I flopped into an armchair in the far corner, I took a picture of the letter on my phone and shoved the letter down deep in my bag once more. Now it would look as if I were reading something on my phone instead of holding a suspicious letter.

Sometimes, I even surprised myself with my genius ideas.

Did you stop reading aloud? I bet you did. Thanks for that. If you can, I'd like you to keep our letters to yourself. And yes, I said 'our' letters. Because this is going to be a two-way street, McKinnon. It's not how the game usually works, but I'm not one to follow all the rules. (That was your first hint, by the way). If I'm going to be writing you all these letters, I want something in return.

Letters. I want info straight from the source. You're going to get to know me, and I want to get to know you. By the time we meet, I want us to feel like we've known each other forever.

Because what I've already seen... the little I already know... I already like. But, I promise I won't be creepy. We'll learn about each other and when we finally meet face to face... it'll be epic.

I promise. I'm known for epic. (Another hint, fyi)

That's it for now. If you accept my terms, write back. Leave the note taped to your locker before school ends today (it doesn't have to be long. Just to let me know you got this and accept).

And tell me.... hmm. Tell me your basics. Favorite color, food, show, movie, etc. Give me a list.

Until tomorrow—
Your Secret Admirer

This feeling coursing through me was new. Was I...swooning? Could I swoon over a letter? Over someone I didn't even know?

Because I totally was.

The tiniest of giggles escaped. I bit down on my bottom lip to keep from being any louder, my cheeks flushing, but not with embarrassment. It was joy.

Glancing around, I checked again to see if anyone was watching me. A group of girls in the corner poured over notebooks and textbooks, most likely studying for a test.

One guy hung out by the door, furiously texting.

And a small semi-circle of guys was opposite me, in the armchairs in the other back corner. None were looking in my direction, but from what I could tell, they were athletes. Baseball, most likely, as two of the four were wearing baseball hats with the Ryder Warrior on it, even though hats weren't allowed during most classes. One of them had a varsity letterman's jacket, a large C on the front left chest for Captain.

Could one of them be my secret admirer?

I turned my attention back to my phone. Thinking about every guy I saw being my mystery man would drive me insane.

Whoever this secret admirer was...was perfect. I had no idea who he was, but he already made me infinitely more comfortable than I was this time yesterday.

This whole game wasn't a game to him at all. It was...ours. Just between him and I. And he wanted me to have an equal part in it.

Given the fact that I didn't know how the whole thing worked otherwise, I had to assume what he was doing was rogue. He said he wasn't a rule follower, so he had to be going against what was normally done.

The little hamster wheel in my head was spinning on overdrive. I needed to write it all down, and quick.

Reaching in my bag for a notebook, I only got as far as finding a pen before the bell rang. My notes would have to wait until after school.

But I had to write back. That I could do while in class.

Rushing to English, I thought about what I would say in my letter. He said he knew some things about me already, but not the basics. I could give him the bare minimum and let him suffer like I was. Or I could be more forthcoming.

My mind debated which to do, clouding my vision as I almost ran into people in the hall. A group of students parted so I could rush past. I threw an apology over my shoulder after I realized what I did.

"Where's the fire?" a deep voice asked as I skidded to a stop outside the English classroom.

A tall, muscular, *popular* guy looked down at me. Like most people, I didn't know his name, but I recognized his face as someone in this class.

"Sorry. Was just...thinking," I mumbled as I pushed past. I peeped over my shoulder and watched as the guy and his friends do their fist bump handshakes before parting.

The guy looked back at me, his slate-gray eyes locking with mine as he strolled into the classroom. My breath hitched and my palms became sweaty.

I broke eye contact first, becoming incredibly self-aware and uncomfortable. I felt his gaze on me as I made my way to my seat, while I pulled open my notebook, and waited for the teacher to start class. He was notoriously always late, so I had a few spare moments.

But before I could start writing...I snuck another peek at the guy with the gray eyes. He was still watching, but not as intensely as before. As soon as he caught me looking back at him, he shifted, pulled out his phone, and began swiping around.

Would I keep looking so suspiciously at every guy this way until I figured out who my secret admirer was? Would every guy become a suspect? Would I ever be able to make friends this month until I solved the mystery?

I couldn't spare the time thinking of all the outrageous scenarios. I had a letter to write.

Dear Secret Admirer—

I accept. I'm not sure why I accept, but your letter seemed to put me at ease more than the first letter did. I have *lots* of questions, but none of them *seem to matter. Yet. But be forewarned—I will ask questions if I need help. And since you insist on me writing back to you, I'll be going straight to the source for those answers. No neutral party for me.*

Accept?

Here's what you wanted to know. There's a story behind almost every one of these answers, and if you're nice, you can get those tales another time.

- *Favorite color: deep violet. An almost black shade of purple.*
- *Favorite food: avocados*
- *Favorite show: none. I like random shows at random times for random moods. It varies.*
- *Favorite movie: The Breakfast Club*
- *Favorite song/artist: again, none. I listen to music based on mood.*
- *Favorite number: 4. For an odd reason, even though it's an even number*
- *Favorite–*

Mr. Caleb walked in just then, making that was the end of my letter. I folded it and put it back in a folder, vowing to steal some tape from somewhere before the school day ended.

And that's exactly what I did. I fashioned an envelope from another piece of paper, grabbed a piece of tape from my last period teacher's desk on my way out, and taped it to my locker.

"What's that?" Skye's voice rang from down the hallway. I groaned, hoping I could escape to the busses without anyone noticing. But Skye was everywhere and into everything.

"Nothing," I replied, gathering my things and shutting the locker.

She raised her eyebrows. "Mhm. And my gran is the Queen. Nothin', my tushie."

I cracked a smile and looped an arm through Skye's. We were the same height when she didn't wear any heels, so today, we came eye to eye.

"I can't tell you," I whispered, keeping my voice low as numerous other students were trying to listen in. Being watched at all times would take a *lot* of getting used to.

Skye huffed. "Excuse *moi*? You can't tell me? Me, of all people? Your bestest friend on the entire planet?" The offensive tone could either be real or fake, I wasn't quite sure which.

I raised my other hand to itch my head. Tonight would have to be a wash night, which meant half an hour of working the curls. It took so long, and my back hurt after, so I only did it once a week usually.

"Nope, sorry. It was in my letter. This entire thing is our secret. He wants me to figure it out on my own." The smile that came after the statement was genuine.

Skye's face crumpled, but she wasn't sad. "Oh my gosh, that's the cutest thing *ever*! And makes me super confused about who it could be now. We were having a debate after you left lunch, but nothing from what you told us added up to anyone we could pinpoint. I was hoping to get more intel from you now, but.... I won't pry. Here if you need help, but *you* are the chosen one, girlfriend. Go slay, little rockstar!"

She ended her speech with a hip check. Approaching the bus lobby, I let go of her arm and waved goodbye.

I kept my eyes peeled, watching every guy that walked by. Would my secret admirer be taking the bus, or did he drive? Was he a junior or a senior? I didn't even think to ask Skye if they could be either class or not.

Tonight, I would go home with almost more questions than I had last night. But tomorrow, I would hopefully come back to another letter. Another secret.

Just for me.

Chapter 7

I wasn't big on social media. I used TikTok mostly for booktok, and Insta for bookstagram. Outside of that, I didn't really care what other people were doing because, until recently, I didn't have a whole lot of people to care *about*.

But with Skye messaging me through Instagram all night last night, begging me to get SnapChat or whatever it was, it made me wonder—would my secret admirer use social media during this game? Were other people talking about me on their social media, outing me as the one chosen for March?

Knowing I was in the spotlight during school hours was strange enough. To think that people talked about me outside of school too was a bit unnerving.

Skye told me not to worry about it, but the looks I was getting on the bus this morning made me think differently.

It didn't take long for word to spread around Ryder High. The second I stepped onto the bus, a hush fell over the students.

"So, what was the first clue?" a random girl who looked younger asked as soon as I sat down. People crowded around me, their eyes wide with expectations, waiting for my answer.

The answer I didn't have. "Um, technically, none? I can't really talk about it..." It was a non-committal answer, and we all knew it. They most likely assumed I was being standoffish or selfish.

"I bet she calls it quits before the end of the week," one person said as they all returned to their seats.

"Yeah, honestly, maybe it's a prank. I mean, she's the new girl. Why would someone choose her?"

"What's with the 'I can't talk about it' deal? Every other girl shares the info freely? Why does she think she's better than the rest?"

"Guys, stop it. You know we're not supposed to judge. If you ever want to be chosen, you have to have good standing."

Good standing? What did that mean? Were people being watched even before they were chosen? Did the ones that threw stones not get picked?

Just how many rules were there with this game?

The last statement from a girl a few rows behind me got everyone to shut up. Instead, the conversation turned to the weekend. I kept an ear open, both wanting to make sure they didn't talk more about me, and also wanting to hear the gossip.

"Leigh, are you going to Connor's party this weekend?"

"I'm not sure. I mean, what's the occasion this time?"

A giggle rippled through the bus. "Does he ever have a reason? It could be the anniversary of his first burp and he'd throw a party. Besides, they're always epic, no matter what the reason. Everyone knows he throws the best parties."

"Yeah, and always has a new girl on his arm every time. Do you think it'll be you, Kennedy? Is that why you're asking? Because let's be honest—no."

Half the bus gasped, the other half hollered at the comment. My eyes widened, hearing the gossip and slander thrown back and forth freely. It seemed light-hearted, but I wasn't always sure.

After another few comments on how hot Connor was, I tuned them out. The way girls could flip the conversation on a dime and pretend nothing else mattered was astounding. I was more laser focused, and had a hard time changing from one topic to another sometimes.

Right when I stepped off the bus, I got attacked again. Skye, plus the entire girl gang from lunch yesterday, was waiting for me. I had hoped that once the excitement wore down, I could go back to getting to my locker and class without being mobbed. Today was not that day.

"There's another note!"

"And a rose!"

"And—oof, ouch!"

Skye pushed her way to the front of the group, giving everyone an evil glare as she did so. "Leave the poor girl alone. Get out of here, all of you!"

She waved her hand, and the group scattered, frowns and groans among them. Spencer glanced back over her shoulder with a thoughtful look on her face, but said nothing.

"Bestie. Can I call you bestie? Great," she continued without getting an answer from me. "So, as they were so rudely spoiling, yes, there's another letter. And yes, a rose. But the rest is a surprise, and it's just for you. Just like the letters. Leave the girls to me. I'll make sure they don't hoard over you like a flock of seagulls to a piece of bread every morning."

She slung her arm over my shoulder, walking down the hall with me a few steps before stopping. "Go. Enjoy. Enjoy the whole process. Don't let what anyone says or does get to you. The girls are either curious or jealous, but neither requires energy from you."

Her smile was the brightest I had yet to see. The crinkle in the corner of her sparkling eyes filled me with excitement as I continued my way to my locker.

They were right. There was another teal envelope and a rose taped to the front.

But below that...

I power-walked down the hall, trying to see what else was on there without looking too ridiculous. My heart leaped into my throat, wondering what was so important.

Swedish Fish.

A bag of Swedish Fish was taped below the note and the rose, a smiley face drawn on the front of one of the picture fish.

And just like that, I started falling for a guy I didn't even know.

I snagged the bag, note, and rose off my locker and opened it, placing each on the shelf gently as I dropped my backpack. I wanted to read the note right here and now, but doing so in public and in a short timeframe didn't seem ideal.

Instead, I switched out my things and closed the locker, making sure to tuck the note and candy inside my bag. I could read it any time today.

I couldn't wait.

*I*t wasn't until third period that I got a moment to read the note. It sat in my bag, and the back of my mind, for hours. Every time I had half a second, I wanted to reach down and grab it.

Modern History was about as boring as it sounded, but we were currently working on individual projects, getting them ready to present to the class in a few weeks. Which meant we could request to go to the library for research instead of staying in class and working.

It worked out perfectly. The moment the teacher came into the room and gave the option, my hand shot into the air. He approved, and I was out the door lickety split.

Settling in an oversized chair in the farthest back corner of the library, I took out my History notebook and the newest letter, leaving the bag of Swedish Fish open, but in my backpack. We weren't allowed to eat in the library, but I could sneak a few out now and then without getting caught.

Unfolding the letter, I took a deep breath. This was real now. *Really* real. Like, not only did a secret admirer send me a letter, but I actually wrote back. We were *communicating.*

Dear McKinnon–

Your note intrigued me. Stories attached to basic information like favorite number? Your favorite color is rather specific as well. Couldn't just be a purple girl, could you?

No, it's good. I like that. It's what makes you unique and interesting. It's what makes you, you. I wouldn't want you to be anyone else.

I figured I'd answer the same questions, so we'd be even. I don't want you thinking that this is a one-sided thing. I wanted equality, and I meant it.

So—

- *Favorite color: Not sure I have a favorite, but currently I'm digging Warrior red...*
- *Favorite food: ballpark hotdogs*
- *Favorite show: Law and Order*
- *Favorite movie: The Sandlot*
- *Favorite music: I'm with you here; whatever I feel like. Today, it's NF*
- *Favorite number: I can't tell you this one. Yet.*

Yes, the above probably gave you some bigger clues than I was expecting to release this early. If you figured it out, congrats. But remember our agreement—you go about this alone. I'm sure if you told any of the other girls, they'd have a roster full of candidates for you to choose from.

But ... I'm being honest here. A bit more ... free (I'm not sure if that's the word I'm looking for, but it's close enough) than I would in person. So, while they may have their ideas, they might not get it right. And if they do figure it out, and compare it to these letters ... well, it wouldn't fit. And it could change the way people see me.

I don't want their perception of me to change. I like the reputation I built here at Ryder. I spent time creating it, and for now I need to keep it. It allows me certain privileges and I'm not afraid to admit that.

But over the years, I've also come to realize there's another part of me that doesn't fit with the image I created. Parts of me that go beyond the guy most people know me as. Hell, even my best friend doesn't know some of the stuff I might be telling you, eventually.

And that's why I wanted to do this month with you. Because with you, I don't have that reputation. I'm a clean slate, an open book, a blank page. I can be whoever I want to be, and so far, I just want to be good enough for you, McKinnon.

Because if you figure out who I am too early ... I'm nervous you might quit. You might think we're not compatible. But I'm here to ask you to give me a chance. Get to know me as the person I want you to see, not the person I am to everyone else. Give the real me a chance. I might surprise you.

Just like your book boyfriends. Speaking of which ... what book are you reading this week?

Leave me a letter,
Your Secret Admirer

Swedish Fish *and* he knew about my book boyfriends? Whoever this guy was, he really did some research. The book was easier to figure out, as I usually had my nose stuck in one, but the Swedish Fish ... that took some digging.

Completely ignoring my History project, I flipped open to a fresh notebook page. I couldn't wait to write back.

Secret Admirer—

You're spot on there. Book boyfriends and Swedish Fish. I'm curious to hear who told you about the Swedish Fish, or if it was a lucky guess.

As for your clues—you aren't going to go about this the typical way, are you? I guess I don't really know what the typical way is, but I assumed it would be a straightforward "here is your next clue". But you're hiding it...

I have some assumptions. I'll make a note of them and see how they stack up against others upcoming.

But I also have some questions. Is this note thing an everyday deal? What if I'm not at school one day, or you're not? What if I don't get my reply to my locker on time?

And what if I figure it out, like, the end of this week? Do I just write back? Would it really be over that quick?

To answer your question, my book of the week is the last book in a ballerina romance series called the On Pointe Series. I should finish it tonight, though, and start a new one tomorrow.

And since you gave me info, I'll end you with this. The reason my favorite color is deep violet is because of the unknown. Most people think that violet is purple (you included, it seems), but it's actually not. Purple is made of equal red and blue. But violet isn't. Actually, humans cannot detect the difference between purple and violet, but some animals can.

But also... it's the last color in the rainbow. Meaning there had to be one hell of a storm and sun to create wavelengths so incredibly powerful to make violet. You don't see it often—the stars of the show are usually red, orange, yellow. Green and blue stand out occasionally, with indigo sliding in there on a rare occasion. But violet, pure violet... it doesn't pop up often.

The stronger your storm, the brighter your rainbow, secret admirer. Remember that.

Until next time
McKinnon

I awoke this morning just like yesterday—expecting another letter on my locker.

But there wasn't one. My locker was blank. No note, no rose, no candy, nothing. I spun the dial on the lock, popping it open with a click, and searching the bottom to see if there was a teal envelope waiting for me.

No luck. For the first time in a few days, there was nothing.

It was just then that I realized how much the letters affected me. They gave me hope, something to look forward to every morning. They had become a bright spot in my day, a part I knew would be there no matter how the rest of the day shaped out.

I had been thinking all night about what he told me in his last letter, and what I wrote back. I wrote more than he did, I think, but I wouldn't take any of it back. It was all important.

I also spent a lot of time picking out any specific details and clues. From Warrior red, ballpark hot dogs, and the Sandlot, I would bet money on the fact that he was on the baseball team.

One quick search of the roster for this spring's baseball team left me with about twenty-five men to choose from. I quickly eliminated the freshman and sophomores, leaving me with a list of eleven. A few of the names jumped out at me from overhearing— Max was in my Spanish class, and Connor, for the party the kids on the bus said they were attending this weekend. Other than that, none of the names meant much, but I put them all down on my list anyway.

Then, he said he couldn't tell me his favorite number. My guess was that it was his jersey number. If he gave me that, he basically gave himself away.

I felt proud of myself. I figured it out all on my own. Of course, it wasn't all that difficult, but I did it. I didn't need any of the other girls' help. A smile crept up my face, just thinking about the secret admirer and the fun we were already having.

"Someone is smiley today," Spencer declared, sliding up to my left and Skye to my right. "Did you get a new letter?"

I shook my head, tucking a few rogue curls behind my ears. Hitching my backpack higher on my shoulders, I gripped the straps with my hands, giving them something to hold on to.

"Actually, no, I didn't. Is that bad?" I said, glancing at both girls.

Skye tucked her lips in, thinking. "I don't think so?

I mean, everyone is different. Most girls got some sort of note or clue each day. But you've already told us you don't think your guy is like most others. So, maybe he doing things different?"

Spencer cocked her head. "What do you mean, different?"

"Oh, McKinnon said that she can't tell us any of the clues. That she has to figure it out on her own."

Spencer came to a dead stop, leaving me and Skye stumbling as we pivoted to face her.

"What? You can't tell anyone the clues? The best part of this whole thing is that everyone is in on it and tries to help figure it out! The best months are when it's more of a school wide thing than an individual thing!"

The frightened look on her face made Skye laugh, but made me nervous. While I had been concerned about other girls being jealous or upset with me being chosen, now I was worried they would react like Spencer.

Would they get mad at me for keeping it all a secret? The original invitation said I could, right? I didn't have to tell anyone anything.

And my secret admirer flat out told me *why* he wanted me to keep it a secret from the other girls. That he had acquired a reputation here at Ryder, but he didn't want me knowing that one. He wanted to show me the real him.

And that alone would ensure I never told a soul about the notes. Not even Skye.

"Get over yourself, Spence. If McKinnon doesn't want to share, she doesn't have to. She was chosen, not you. Besides, at the latest, you'll find out when she figures it out, or at the end of the month."

Spencer's mouth gaped open. "But...but..."

"No buts, darling. Unless it's Austin's over there, be-cause honestly, that's a *peach*," Skye replied, slipping her hand through my arm and pointing to a guy on the other side of the hallway. His back was to us, but he was tall with short brown hair, and yes, had quite the ass on him. He stood among a group of guys. Only one was facing us though—another tall guy with a buzz cut, brown hair, and wearing a varsity letterman jacket. The one with the C on it, from the student union the other day.

I looked up at him, but he diverted his eyes before I could catch them, turning back to join his friend's conversation.

Spencer cleared her throat, straightened her shoul-ders, and continued on. "Well then, fine. Keep your secrets. I'm sure it'll all come out soon, anyway. Secrets never last long around here, especially ones related to the secret admirers."

My heart dropped. Was she right? Would people some-how find out?

I turned to Skye, panic stricken. "Skye. What if some-one stole the letter off my locker this morning?"

A small smile crossed her lips. "Not saying it hasn't happened before, but I highly doubt it. I'm sure you've figured out by now that the boys somehow keep track of girls who are catty or nice about the whole thing, right?"

I nodded, having deduced the same thing, but didn't confirm it until now. There was so much about this game that I was clueless about. Things that could potentially hinder my participation.

"Well, if they caught someone stealing your note, that person would automatically be disqualified from ever being chosen. That alone usually keeps people away."

"What if a *guy* took it, though? A straight guy, I mean," I corrected myself, remembering her whole inclusivity speech the other day. "How could they punish him?"

"He would never be allowed to participate as an admirer, would he? McKinnon, honestly, don't worry or think too much into the details. This has been going on for years and years now, and the entire student body is behind it. It's never gotten out of hand, and even the teachers sometimes like to be a part. It's meant to be fun."

I sucked in a deep breath, still worked up and freaked out. It was supposed to be fun, she said. And most of the time, when I was reading the letters, it *was* fun.

But there was no letter today.

I was deep into fourth period when a knock on the door startled just about everyone in the class.

The teacher opened it, sticking her head out instead of letting the person in. We all strained our heads to see who she was talking to, but it was no use.

I turned back to my desk, drumming my pencil on my textbook. Everything seemed duller without a letter to look forward to reading. In such a short time, I had gotten my hopes up about learning more about this guy, and today, I was a deflated balloon.

"McKinnon?" my teacher asked, causing me to snap my head up and stare at the front of the room. "You seem to have a delivery. A *secret* delivery," she added with a wink. "It's just outside."

After cocking her head toward the door, the lightbulb went off in my head. I had to go out to get it. Which meant getting up in having the entire class watch while I made a spectacle of myself.

Ducking my head, I pushed up my glasses and headed toward the front, not looking at anyone in the process. I opened the door and slipped out, closing it behind me quickly.

A cellophane wrapped basket with a torso and legs greeted me.

"Um, hi?" I said, trying to see who was behind the basket. Finally, he lowered it and pushed it out to me.

It was the guy from my English class. The one I still didn't know the name of with the gray eyes that stared intensely and short, cropped blonde hair.

"This is for you. It's not from me. Don't get any ideas."

I accepted the basket, cradling it under one arm. "What's your name?" It slipped out before my brain caught up.

The guy shook his head, his eyes narrowing as if the question itself was a bother. Or maybe this whole delivery thing was a bother.

"Owen," he replied. Just as quickly as he answered, he turned and started down the hallway without another word or a glance back.

My cheeks flushed a deep shade of red as I ducked back into the classroom, again trying to avoid all eye contact. The basket wasn't huge by any means, but completely noticeable, especially when I was as on display as it was.

I hurried back to my seat, shoving the basket under my legs. I barely looked at it when Owen handed it to me. The contents were a mystery, but I had high hopes it was from my secret admirer.

The first thing I did was make a mental note to ask if I could call him by some other name. "Secret Admirer" was fun and all, but a nickname of sorts would be easier in letters.

"Looks like someone is having fun with this month's secret admirer game," my teacher whispered as she walked by while passing out the homework for tonight. I gulped, nodded, but couldn't squeak out any actual words.

Skye said some teachers enjoyed being in on the game, and she seemed like one of them.

She didn't mention it for the rest of class, but gave me another knowing smile as I rushed out of the room once the bell rang. I was starving and lunch was next.

But first, I wanted to dig into this basket.

Chapter 10

"We heard about your present," Skye practically sang as she popped over my shoulder and wrapped an arm around me.

I jumped, startled by her sudden appearance.

"So, where is it?" she asked, rounding around and facing me from the front. I was approximately three steps away from my locker, but she was blocking me.

Instead of answering, I pointed behind her. She spun around, took in her surroundings, and chuckled. "Whoops."

"I didn't open it yet, if that was going to be your next question," I said, pushing past her and spinning the combination. I meant to find a place to open it before going to the cafeteria earlier, but just carrying it down the hallway caused the whispers and finger points to start up again. In the end, I ditched it in my locker, rushed to the cafeteria, and didn't even mention it to anyone.

Skye nodded. "It was. And why not?"

I shrugged. "Haven't had a spare moment yet. It's not something I can really lug around and open whenever." I left out the part about the gossiping. Skye would worry, and if she worried, she took action. The last thing I wanted was more people talking about me.

Skye paused, her gaze ping-ponging between me and the basket teetering on the tops of my textbooks. "I would go absolutely *bonkers* if I had to wait so long!"

She waited another beat, as if she wanted to ask something else, but held back. Which was unlike her, so she had to be showing some massive restraint. It made me proud.

Since she promised not to pry, and to keep others from prying, she really was holding to it, as much as it probably pained her.

"I'm opening it at home. Sorry," I answered her unasked question. Her face fell, crumpling from her forehead down in what seemed like slow motion.

I knew this whole secrecy thing was killing her inside, but I couldn't help it. Even if the secret admirer guy didn't ask for me to keep it to myself, I wasn't sure how much I would share. Maybe a few of the clues, so they could point me in the right direction, but would I read every note aloud? Probably not. Would I share every detail? Most likely not.

Skye took a deep breath and plastered a smile back on her face. "That's alright. I have a different question for you."

I hoisted my bag onto my shoulder and leaned down to reach for the basket. Standing up, I shut my locker with my foot and stared at my friend.

"Want a ride home with me so you don't have to take that on the bus?"

My eyes widened. Skye lived on the opposite side of town from me, making it difficult to carpool. To not have to take the basket on the bus, in front of more prying eyes, would be amazing.

I narrowed my eyes for a moment, sizing her up. "You're not expecting me to open the basket in the car, are you?"

She threw her hands in the air, palms toward me. "No, of course not. Okay, fine, I'm a bit excited about it, but I totally respect your privacy. I promise. But if you happen to peek inside while I drive and want to share..."

We started down the hall as I shook my head. "We'll see."

After settling in the passenger seat of Skye's light blue sedan, my backpack settled between my legs and the basket on my lap, she started the car and backed out of the parking spot.

The main reason I had yet to determine what was inside was the fact that he wrapped the contents. The basket was white, woven wicker, and each item was wrapped in plain brown paper. The entire thing had cellophane around it, tied at the top with a ribbon.

Either my secret admirer was one heck of a gift-wrapper, or he had some help. My bet was on the latter, but it was anyone's guess.

"What do you think is inside? Did he give any clues as to what he may give you?" Skye asked, flipping on her turn signal to head toward my house.

"I don't think so? His clues haven't been super straight forward. They've been more ... embedded inside the letters," I said, thinking back to what his last one said. Did he mention something that would give the contents away? Did *I* mention something that would determine what it was?

"I think it's adorable that he's writing you letters instead of just dropping clues," Skye replied, taking another right turn.

I looked at her. "Is that not normal? I mean, I've gathered as much, but what is the game like usually?" There were so many questions still left unanswered, but I didn't care about it as much. My secret admirer and I were playing as we wanted to play; how anyone else did it didn't matter.

I was still curious and wanted to know all the information I could, even if it didn't fully apply.

Skye glanced over her shoulder before changing lanes, then replied. "I guess it changes? The guys can play however they want, as long as there are clues given and a way for the recipient to figure out who they are before months end. For the most part, though, the guy leaves a trail of clues. Sometimes that's in a letter, sometimes it's in a scavenger type hunt, or sometimes it's delivered by different people each time. It varies, but the full-on letter writing is the first I've heard of. And it's so freaking cute."

She didn't even know about me writing letters back. If him writing me letters instead of just dropping clues was different, then she really would freak out if she knew about me writing back. My secret admirer and I were becoming pen pals of sorts, and that had to be a first.

Skye pulled into my driveway and shut off the engine for a moment. I gathered my things before opening the door, but paused before I got out.

"Thanks for the ride. I appreciate it. Lugging this on the bus, with everyone watching, really didn't sound like fun," I said, giving her a genuine smile.

"No problem. I hope you like what's inside," she replied with a signature Skye grin.

I hoped so too. I couldn't wait to get in and rip it open.

Chapter 11

Only Mom was home when I got inside, but thankfully she was in the shower, so I could sneak up to my room without her seeing the basket.

Trying to explain to her what the secret admirer thing was all about would be over her head. She wasn't too keen on me attending Ryder High as it was, and this would send her over the edge.

Mom had homeschooled me my entire life until a few months ago. When Dad's job suddenly got transferred to a new state, she didn't have time to get all the requirements and testing set up before I had to begin school again.

Plus, I sort of petitioned to go to regular school. It was hard enough staying home freshman, sophomore, and half of junior year, while everyone else I knew went to public school. It was time to take the plunge and try it out.

But Ryder High had an excellent rating in all categories, Mom talked extensively to the principal before I started, and finally caved. And I got to attend public school for the first time ever.

The last thing I expected when I started was a school wide monthly mystery. It was like nothing I read about in any books about high schoolers, or any shows I watched on any streaming service. It was completely mind-boggling when Skye first mentioned it just a few days ago, but now...I was all in.

Dumping my backpack on my desk chair, I practically threw myself onto my bed, cradling the basket in my hands and checking it out before I opened it.

After undoing the ribbon, I slipped the basket out of the plastic wrap and laid it on the bed carefully.

There were four items wrapped in the brown paper. One I was sure was a book. The other three were mysteries.

I opened the book first. If my secret admirer got me one I had yet to read, and in my preferred genre, it would earn the most brownie points ever.

Slipping my finger under the tape, I carefully removed the brown paper, making sure I opened it up to the back cover first, so I didn't spoil the surprise.

Without Merit, by Colleen Hoover, stared at me when I flipped it over, and my heart dropped to my stomach.

Oh, he was good. He was *really* good. Scary good, actually. How he knew I had wanted this book for a while now was beyond me.

I flipped through the pages, the character names jumping out at me. I stopped and stared at the cover again, running my fingers over the words and tracing the letters.

After giving the book a quick hug, I set it on the bed next to me and dove back into the basket. Right where the book had been was an envelope. A teal envelope. It must have been hidden under the book, because I hadn't seen it before.

I tore into it, not even caring that I was ripping the beautiful envelope in half.

McKinnon—

Let me guess. You opened the book first? Because you knew it would be a book based on the shape and size, and it intrigued you the most. You would have had to open the book to find this envelope.

And now you're blushing. Your cheeks are getting that pink tinge I think is adorable.

It was like he was here in the room with me, watching my every move. A shiver ran through me, but not the bad kind.

He called me adorable. And I liked it.

Did you open the rest of them yet? If you haven't, put the letter down and do so now. I'll wait (lol, I mean, where am I going to go as a piece of paper?)

He didn't need to tell me twice. I dropped the note, letting it flutter to the floor as I reached for the next item in the basket.

Not caring about the paper this time, I ripped it to shreds trying to get what was inside. This smaller item was only a few inches by a few inches, a tiny little thing.

It was a canvas. A small canvas painting, to be exact.

Of a bunch of violets in a black vase, against the starry sky.

Oh. My. Word. How did he come up with this in less than a day? The emotions running through me right now were on a level I had never experienced before.

I never experienced much with boys before, period. And to have one lavishing me with gifts I already loved, and sweet words of affirmations...

He hit all my love languages, and I highly doubt he knew what love languages even were.

There were two more items in the basket, and I couldn't contain my excitement at opening them. The only downside to this entire thing was the fact that I was sitting here, alone, unable to share the enthusiasm with anyone else.

Sure, I could call Skye, and FaceTime her while I opened. But that would break the promise I made in our first letter.

I couldn't even properly thank him. Because so far, gifts like these required a physical thank you in the form of a hug. And seeing we were only a few days into our month-long mystery...that was out of the question.

The next package was smaller than the book, but larger than the canvas. The paper tore off with ease, as if he knew I would be getting impatient the further into the basket I went.

The label on the box gave the item away. *The Smell of Books* Soap Company stared back at me.

"The scent of paper from an old, dusty paperback found on the back shelf, forgotten and dejected, mixed with the cedarwood every book boyfriend seems to wear, with a hint of mint," I read out loud, almost unable to finish as I burst out laughing. I lifted it to my nose, taking a sniff. Pleasantly surprised, it was delicious. If I had my candle lighter closer, I would definitely light it.

But I had one more item to unpack. Placing the candle next to the book and canvas, I grabbed the last one and went to town, throwing the paper over my shoulder. It was like Christmas morning all over again.

A notebook. A small, purse sized notebook. The cover had details of purple, pink, and blue watercolors mixed together. I opened the cover, finding writing already on the first page.

> *To write all your thoughts and dreams.*
> *And clues. Mostly the clues.*

A smiley face followed the note. I huffed out a laugh, but he was right. It would be convenient to put all my notes about who he was in one place, especially one that was as small and portable as this. Jotting them down on whatever was in front of me would guarantee that something got lost over time.

Reaching over to my nightstand, I grabbed a pen and clicked it open. Before I even picked up the letter again, I wrote the items in my memory down on the second page of the notebook, leaving the first with only his words.

After I finished, I leaned down and grabbed the note, starting it from where I left off.

I hope you like them all. Just a few things I found that reminded me of you. I will say, so you don't think I'm a huge stalker, that I found the book on your (public) Amazon wish list. I saw it there the other day and tracked it down at that independent bookstore over on 5th Avenue. The canvas, well… that's a story for another time.

The candle and the notebook were from the bookstore too. They jumped out at me and I had to get them. Don't think too much into it… I mean, I hope it's okay that I got you some gifts. I just saw them and when I got the book and thought you would like them.

So, for your clues today… if you haven't already seen, well, then you'll find them. They're in there. I'll be waiting patiently for when you do. No rush.

Good Luck
Your Secret Admirer

PS—sorry about Owen. I'm sure he was obnoxious when he delivered this. Don't worry, he's not always that grumpy and annoying.

I flipped the paper over, expecting something more. There was nothing for me to reply to today. No question he asked, nothing he wanted to know. Plus, the school day was already long over and I didn't leave a note for him.

Frowning, I put the note on top of everything else and looked at the basket. A bit of crumpled-up brown paper, the same as the wrapping of the gifts, laid on the bottom, used to support the items. I grabbed it and tossed it aside, looking for something underneath, but coming up empty.

The basket sat empty in my hands. There was nothing written on it, nothing else inside. So what did he mean?

The paper. The crumpled-up paper. Maybe there were more clues written on those? I chucked the basket at my pillows and grabbed the paper, flattening them out on top of the book.

But again, I came up empty. There was nothing there, on either side.

Sighing, I gave up for the time being. I had to eat dinner, do my homework, and study for an Algebra test in the morning. I couldn't let this thing take over my entire life. It was fun, I made me happy, and whoever the guy was, he was growing on me, fast.

But I had to stick to my priorities. School came first. If I started slipping, Mom would pull me and bring me home again, where she could control exactly what I learned and at what pace.

And after this past week, that was the *last* thing I wanted.

*B*efore I left the house, I slipped the book in my bag, vowing to read it on the bus. I also dropped the small notebook inside, with my clues and questions carefully written down.

The candle and the canvas sat on my desk, waiting for another time.

"There she is! The chosen one!" someone yelled as I climbed the steps of the bus. My head whipped up, my glasses sliding down my nose, as I looked to see who called. Given the secret admirer news wasn't, well, new, it surprised me.

A bunch of people in the back started clapping, and I wasn't sure why. I gave a shy wave and made my way to my seat, hoping no one would come over to bother me.

Surprisingly, that's exactly what happened. Not a single person came over. No one leaned over the seat in front or behind me, no one slid on the bench next to me, and no one made another comment.

It was all so perplexing. This entire thing was mind-boggling.

"They were warned," a voice called from my right. The guy who sat across from me, the same one who made sure I got off at my stop the other day, gave me a reassuring smile.

My brows furrowed. "Warned?"

His blue eyes shone with glee, matching the bright smile. "Yup. Word spread about you being the new 'it girl', but the word attached to it was to leave you alone. That this month was solely for you, and no one was to help you or bother you about it. Of course, that doesn't stop most people from cheering you on, as seen back there." He jabbed a thumb over his shoulder, indicating the students behind us.

"Who warned them?" I questioned, confused about the whole thing. My letter said I was to keep it to myself, but there was never any mention of someone telling the rest of the student body. And whoever did, must have done it last night, as Skye didn't say anything about it when we drove home yesterday.

The guy shrugged. "I don't know. Who really knows with these things? All it takes is a few people to get the word and be told to push it out, and with the power of texts and social media, it gets to people."

That's why I didn't hear about it. Not only did I not use social media that much, but being new, not many people would have even found me. Once again, I wondered if it would hinder me in some way during this month, and it seemed as if it already took its toll.

"By the confused look on your face, I'm assuming you didn't get the memo?"

I shook my head. "I mean, no, but yes? It's complicated, I guess. By the way, I'm McKinnon."

He shot me a look that told me he obviously knew that already, and my face flushed. I hated that my cheeks turned bright red at every little embarrassment.

"I'm Colby. It's nice to officially meet you, McKinnon." He took one hand and pushed the dark shaggy hair off his forehead while giving me another dazzling smile. "Do you mind?" He pointed to the spot next to me, and I silently replied by moving over a few inches toward the window.

Colby slid over seamlessly. As soon as he joined me, the aroma of his cologne had me in stitches.

"Cedarwood and mint?" I asked, holding back a deep belly laugh.

"Yes..." he trailed off. It had to be confusing why I was trying not to burst out laughing.

"Sorry. I just got a candle that was a mix of cedarwood and mint," I tried to explain, knowing that it would make no sense to him, but also not caring. He had been warned as well, which meant I didn't have to tell him who gave me the candle.

Colby just shook his head and smiled again. His smile was calming and held no expectations, which was nice.

And now that I knew the entire student body had been told off, the anxiety rushing through me seemed to have vanished as well. No longer did I fear people seeing a note on my locker or someone looking at me, waiting to pounce with questions. Knowing they were supposed to leave me alone gave me more freedom to explore the whole mystery myself.

"So, do you have any idea who your mystery guy is yet?" Colby asked as we disembarked the bus. We walked side by side through the lobby and down the first hallway.

"I thought you weren't supposed to ask?"

He huffed out a small laugh. "Well, yeah, I guess. I'm not trying to pry or help you if you don't want. But curiosity killed the cat, ya know?"

I grinned. I could tell that he wasn't jealous like some others, or upset that I had been chosen and wasn't going to release any information from the letters. He seemed genuinely curious. I didn't know why, but I felt like I could trust him. Not that I would give him any real information; definitely nothing more than I would tell Skye.

She would be so pissed off if she found out I was telling a stranger more information about the secret admirer than I told her.

"I have a few clues so far. Narrowed down the field a bit," I mentioned casually. "I don't know many people here at Ryder High, so it'll make it a bit more difficult, but it seems like he took that into account. But no, I have no idea. And ... I kind of hope I don't figure it out for a while, you know?"

Colby nodded, but stopped walking as we got to an intersection. "I get it. You want the fun to last. I gotta jet this way, but see you on the bus this afternoon?"

I grinned. "Yeah. I'll be there."

If the only good thing to come out of this whole mystery secret admirer thing was the fact that people were talking to me like a real person and wanting to be my friend ... I'd call it a win.

*T*he morning passed without any problems. There was nothing on my locker when I arrived, no one standing around pretending to keep busy while they watched me, and nothing happened in any of my first few classes.

"What's wrong?" Spencer asked as I joined the lunch table. It was only her and Skye today; the rest of the girls must have thought I wasn't cool enough to hang out with now that I wasn't freely giving out information.

"Nothing," I replied, poking at my applesauce.

Skye nudged my shoulder, urging me to continue. I sighed, took a sip of milk, and rested my chin on my palm.

"There was no note today," I muttered. The second it left my lips, I felt like an idiot. Why I was expecting there to be something for me every day, I didn't know. Until a few days ago, I would die of embarrassment if there was something taped to my locker.

But now... I wanted to hear from him. Even though I had enough things from the gift basket last night to tide me over for a while. They were unexpected, thoughtful, and way beyond what I thought the scope of the game was.

I was already being spoiled, and it was getting to me. It wasn't that I wasn't grateful; I really, really was. But I was also becoming trained to expect something from him every day.

Which was crazy. Especially because I hadn't written back yet.

"Well, did you figure out the last clues? Maybe that has something to do with what's coming next?" Spencer asked. Her wavy brown hair sat in two French braids that hung down her back and her bright green eyes shone behind a pair of tortoiseshell glasses I had never seen before. I had no idea if they were for actual vision correctness or not, but they were cute on her.

I bit my lip, staring down at my uneaten food. "Not really..."

"Were there even clues in that basket? It looked more like presents," Skye asked while munching on a French fry.

Taking a deep breath, I lowered my head into my folded arms on the table. The softness of my sweatshirt comforted me, but didn't bring any answers. "Kinda. At least, he said there were, but I didn't find them. I'm not sure what to do, but I'll figure it out."

Before either of them could speak, a thought popped into my head. "Did you guys get the notice to not ask me about anything? The warning?" I looked up at them from beneath my eyelashes and over the top of my glasses. They were blurry, but I could make out their sheepish facial expressions just fine.

"Well...yeah. But you're our friend, so we figured...um...," Skye stuttered.

Spencer interrupted her. "We figured it didn't really apply to us. I mean, I know I'm not as close to you as Skye is, but whatever. We're friends now. And if you wanted to tell us, you would. And if you need help, we're here. But we're also here as friends. This is a new experience for you. We want to be there for you through it all. And if that means you're feeling happy or sad or anything between, we want you to know that our ears are open, and our shoulders are ready for you to lean on."

My jaw dropped. She said it all so matter-of-factly, as if it was clear as day to everyone.

"Yeah," Skye chimed in, "what she said."

Friends. Friends that didn't care about my secret admirer. Friends who were going to be there for me regardless of the results, it seemed like.

"Thanks, guys," I mumbled, sitting up a little straighter now. "I'm a little stumped on this last part, that's all. I'm sure I'll figure it out. And if I don't, I promise, you two will be the first ones I ask."

"Perfect," Spencer replied. "And Skye will keep pretending she's not dying to know what was inside that basket."

Skye scrunched her nose. "Is it that obvious?"

Spencer threw a French fry in her direction. "Only to anyone that knows you."

I laughed and decided then to give them a little something. "I'll tell you one thing. One of the gifts was a book. He stalked me enough to realize I have a public Amazon wish list, saw the title, and found it at the little book store on 5th Avenue."

Skye's eyes widened. "That's adorable!" She drew out the letters, adding a flair at the end of adorable. "Ugh, McKinnon, this whole thing is just the cutest!" Like the Mouse she was, her voice rose as she continued speaking.

Several people around us turned their heads, looking to see what she was getting excited about. I shushed her as quick as I could and Spencer threw another fry at her.

"Geesh, Skye, alert the entire cafeteria next time, would you?" Spencer muttered through gritted teeth.

Though I didn't know Spencer as well as Skye, I liked her. She was a no-nonsense type of person, which balanced Skye quite well.

"I'm gonna go," I said, gathering up my things. I wanted to see if I could get a few minutes of reading in before the bell rang. My entire reading list moved aside so I could start this book today. There had to be a reason he chose it, and I wanted to see why.

"Hit us up if you need us!" Skye shrieked before I left the cafeteria. I waved over my shoulder, not daring to look back and see everyone staring now.

Instead of heading to the union like I did to read the first letter, I headed toward my English class. I could sit in the hallway outside the classroom. It would cut down on the commute and give me more time to dive into the book.

Settling in on the floor a few feet away from the door, I got the book out of my bag, smiling when I saw the notebook next to it. I had nothing new to add to it, but seeing it just made me happy.

I breathed in, smelling the freshness of the pages and ink. The initial crack of the spine as I opened the cover sent chills up my spine. There was nothing better than being the first person to open a brand-new book and break it in.

Except I wasn't the first person to open it.

The title page had writing on it. And not a signature from the author.

No, this writing was similar to the handwriting on the notes I'd been receiving.

It was my secret admirers writing.

> *Surprise! If you've found this, congrats on finding today's clue. Actually, this may be considered the clues for a few days, because there's going to be a handful of them here. It depends on how fast you read, I suppose. Enjoy the book...*

The book held the clues. He said it was in the basket and he wasn't lying. I just didn't look hard enough. If I had only cracked open the book last night, I would have figured it out.

Laughing to myself, I flipped to the next page and began reading. The second page gave way to the first hint.

"Fail my driver's test," was underlined in black pen.

I immediately dug into my bag and grabbed the notebook, transferring the sentence under my other clues.

Whoever this guy was, he was most likely on the baseball team and failed his driver's test. It didn't rule out everyone, but it certainly narrowed the field.

Too bad I wouldn't continue my search into who he was until I finished the book. There were bound to be more clues inside.

Besides, the book itself was amazing. The more I read, the more I got sucked in. The mystery could wait.

Three days later, I finished reading. My notebook was littered with clues and things he had underlined. I read every moment I could—between classes, skipping lunch, and at home. Still, between enjoying the book and finding the clues, it took me three days. It didn't stop the whispers during those three days, though. I learned to overlook them, but I could tell people were talking. Seeing a teal envelope taped to my locker was the universal sign that I was still in the game, and without it, the rumors swirled. Since I knew the truth, I didn't let them get to me this time.

The biggest question I had over the past three days was *how* my secret admirer read and annotated the book so fast. The only reasonable explanations were that he had read it before, was a faster reader than I was, or got it before the month started.

It killed me to not be able to ask, but I wanted to wait until I finished the book to write a letter back. As a gentleman, I suspected he was waiting for my letter before he sent another one.

As I read, I collected clues in the notebook and kept a separate page for questions and things I wanted to include in my letter to him. Quotes I liked from the book that I thought he might like too, questions about themes I picked up on that I wanted this opinion on, and some about what he underlined or annotated.

In all, I had pages of clues on him, yet none of them added up. They ranged from things like the word trophy being underlined numerous times to "little sister" being circled and a broken heart next to it.

All of the things together made no sense. Separate, I could try to figure them out, but they were too out of place to belong to just one person. At least, with my limited knowledge of the guys of Ryder High.

Instead, just before shutting down for the night, I pulled out a pen and a bigger piece of paper than from the little notebook, and started writing. I didn't refer to my notes or any of the things I had written down about the book.

I just wrote what was in my head. My true, in the moment thoughts and feelings.

Dear Secret Admirer—

First, I would like to officially request a nickname. The term 'secret admirer' is outdated and, like you've said before, a bit unsettling. You're not creepy, but the term makes me shudder. So please, if you will, send a new name I can address these letters to.

Second... the gifts... were perfect. Way too much, but perfect. I wasn't expecting anything at all, and definitely not items like those. I don't blame you for peeking into my wish list—though, now that you see what I read, I hope you don't judge me. Romance books are for everyone, alright?

Of course, you seem to know that. Because you did your homework. Annotating a book for a girl? Taking a page out of Jess Mariano's book, are you? (If you get the reference, please tell me!) I need to know—how long ago did you read it?

I'll admit, it was smart. I wish I would have had time to crack the book open the night I got it, but it wasn't until the next day that I realized. Hiding clues inside a book? All things that don't make too much sense, but I'm sure you've worked out how to piece them all together.

I already have a list of potential names of who you are. I've gotten the baseball thing figured out, as well as the driver's license. The other big clues are little sister.... But the broken heart is throwing me off. In my heart, I think it's a sad reason, but I don't want it to be sad. Because I don't want that kind of sadness in your life.

Anyway, thank you for the gifts. The candle is wonderful, the notebook has come in handy often, and the canvas is beautiful. I would love to hear the story behind it, whenever you want to tell me.

I'll leave you with another little diddy about me. The reason the Breakfast Club is my favorite movie is odd. The house I grew up in, the one I lived at until we moved here, was down the street from the school where they filmed the movie. It's a Sheriff's station now, for the state police, but back then it was a high school. There really is a gym too. Mom says they had a program for kids back in the nineties and they used the gym all the time. No word if the library is still there.

But yes, I grew up driving by that circular drive in the front, looking at the steps and wondering if that building still held secrets left behind by the members in detention. It's silly, I know.

I'm not sure what else to say. I have a whole list of notes and questions in my new notebook... but this letter isn't for them. This one is all me, straight to you. I don't know what other things to tell you, because I'm not sure what you know and what you don't.

And I want to learn more about you. More than little clues and hints. I feel like I don't know you at all, but also like I've known you for years. It's a weird, battling feeling inside of me.

Here's a tidbit. I have a scar right where my eyebrow starts on my right side. When I was twelve, my friend and I were messing around, and I fell. My glasses smashed into my face and cut me. My friend's mom freaked out, but all I needed was a butterfly bandage, no stitches. But the scar is still there.

Do you have any scars?

Until next time—
McKinnon

Before I put the letter in an envelope, I added one more page—the paper I doodled quotes and thoughts on. It was a little something I loved to do while reading, and for some reason, I thought he may like it. It wasn't a page directly full of hand written quotes, it had a more artistic look to it, with little pictures of trophies, a church, and other scribbles among it. They were fun to make and to look back on when I thought about a certain book.

After stuffing both the letter and the doodle in an envelope, I made sure to pack a roll of tape so I could adhere it to my locker first thing in the morning.

I went to bed with a smile on my face, a little bit giddy about tomorrow. I hated making him wait so long for my letter, and only hoped he replied quicker than I did.

Dear McKinnon—

A nickname, huh? I guess it could be weird saying secret admirer all the time. I think I'm used to it, since I've been at Ryder and am a part of this group, but I can see how it would be odd for you.

So what about... how about a real name? It's my second middle name, and not a single soul on this planet besides family members knows it. Honestly, I'm not even sure anyone outside my house would even realize it if someone told them.

It's Charlie. So, for now, you can call me Charlie. Unfortunately, it won't help your search at all, but maybe it'll ease your mind a bit.

Moving on. I'm glad you liked the gifts. I'll admit—I read the book a week or so ago. Then I went back to the bookstore for the candle and notebook, after reading your first letter to me. You seemed like a notebook type of person, someone who likes to write down her thoughts and keep it all together.

The canvas...I guess I can tell you now. I painted it. Like my second middle name, I don't believe anyone knows I paint. Most of my friends would laugh if you told them I did it. They don't think I'm skilled in areas outside of athletics, but jokes on them. Your favorite color inspired it.

One of the reasons I wanted to join this group and do this with you is because of secrets. I have a lot of them. Like I told you before, most people at Ryder see me in one way.

But I want you to see me another way. The real me. The parts that I hide from everyone else.

Maybe it's selfish. Maybe it's stupid of me to think that I could be someone else. That you wouldn't pass judgment since you don't know me yet.

But I wanted to try. And, once you find out who I am, if you want nothing to do with me in person, that's fine. This entire game is your choice. You call the shots. You make the plays. As soon as you accepted the invitation, the ball was in your court, and I'm following your lead.

Just know...the McKinnon I see from afar completely matches the McKinnon I see in your letters. To me, you are one and the same. A girl I like, both inside and out.

I just hope you give me the same chance at the end of the month.

Can't wait to hear from you again—
"Charlie"

PS. Scars—yeah, I have a handful. Mostly from being stupid with a bunch of "watch this" moments when I was younger. My last one I got last year, though. It's in the same places as yours, right by my eyebrow. The seam of the baseball ripped my skin open. I turned down stitches, but it was bloody and gross. In hindsight, that was a dumb idea, but the idea of the needle was worse than a scar at the time.

I had to wait two days for this letter.

And I knew why.

Here was a boy, pouring his heart out to a stranger. Someone he had no idea what thoughts were going through her head, if she liked him the same way he liked her. To him, I was a stranger of sorts, someone he begged to be accepted by based solely on his letters.

His letters took thought. They bled emotion and feelings not usually found in a seventeen-year-old guy. They took time because he skillfully crafted them to be a mixture of true thoughts and carefree verse.

And I'd be damned if I ever for one second judged him for being something other than who he was in those letters.

I added the note about his scar, the painting, his name, and even how his personality would be different when I searched into my notebook, then rushed to write a reply.

Charlie—

Much better. Addressing a letter to a real name makes it feel like I'm not talking to a random stranger anymore.

I wanted to thank you again. Thank you for being real in your letters. For not taking the easy way out and dropping a clue and being done with it.

I can tell you take your time with what you write. That every word on the page is real and true and deeply you.

And, I can tell you, without a doubt, I like what I read. Even if I figure out who you are, it won't change anything. It would be like judging a book by its cover, right? Sure, we all do it. Pretty covers draw you in, they make you pick up the book.

But the words inside can be horrendous. The plot could suck, the characters could be underdeveloped, and the villain should be the hero.

Sometimes, though, the plainest covers have the best stories. And you, Charlie, have an amazing story. It doesn't matter to me what your cover is. Your story is uniquely yours and there's nothing more I'd rather read at the moment.

In fact, your letters have stopped my TBR entirely. Obviously, it shot Without Merit straight to the top, pushing back every other book that I've had waiting. They're a bit mad about that, but I told them to take it up with you.

But your letters have become my reading material. And you have become a book boyfriend.

Dear McKinnon

That's weird. I don't even know you and I just called you a book boyfriend.

It's true though. You really would make a good one.

My tidbit for you tonight—my favorite book of all time is The Sea of Tranquility by Katja Millay. Josh Bennett is an excellent book boyfriend.

—McKinnon

I noticed a change in me over the past week. Well, since this entire game started, really. Whereas I used to hide and stay out of the way, I now stood out. And for once, I was alright with that.

I walked down the hallways with my head up, smiling almost all the time, waving hello to people who greeted me. It wasn't so intimidating anymore, to be the center of attention.

Besides, the one thing I did was keep an eye out. I wanted to see if I could find someone with a scar by their eyebrow, especially one of the baseball guys. But they were a hard group to get attention from—most of them were the most popular guys. And while the thought crossed my mind that Charlie could be one of them, I doubted it.

Sure, he wanted me to know him for who he was in his letters and not who the rest of the school saw him as. But my list was still hovering around ten names—half of them were the popular guys, and the other half were just regular people.

"Macks!" Skye's shrill voice echoed in the hallway as I made my way to the bus. "I need your help!"

I paused, waiting for her to catch up. "What's up?"

She stopped, placing her hands on her knees and panting. "I need an extra hand. I have to take photos of the marsh out back and write some notes, and I literally don't have enough hands for it all."

I scrunched my brow. "The marsh? Now?"

The marsh took up a good portion of the back acreage of the school's property, and it was mainly used for science classes and P.E. Sometimes, in the winter, the P.E. classes would go snow shoeing around there, once the ground was frozen and there was enough snow.

But the snow had melted and spring was right around the corner, which meant at this moment, it was a cold, muddy mess.

Skye turned on her best puppy dog pleading face, batting her lashes at me and whimpering for extra effect. "Please? I'll drive you home after?"

I sighed, glancing out toward my bus, watching Colby climb aboard. He had been out sick the past few days, and I hadn't had a chance to talk to him. Last week, I convinced him to grab a copy of *Without Merit*, and was desperate to know his thoughts. I didn't tell him about Charlie reading it, though.

"I guess," I moaned, voicing my displeasure about the fact. "If my shoes get destroyed out there, you're buying me a new pair."

"Deal," Skye agreed, sticking out her hand to shake

on it. "Can you carry the notebook and pen? The strap on my camera broke, so I have to hold it the entire time."

We made small talk on our way out to the marsh, and after twenty minutes, we both had enough. Between the thawing plants and the stagnant water, our noses were deeply affected. Skye got enough pictures and notes for her class, so we headed back toward the parking lot.

"Oh! They started!" Skye exclaimed as we made our way down the path.

"Who started what?"

She pointed across the field, toward a baseball diamond not too far away. "The varsity boys. Some of them come out before official practices begin, to get a head start. As soon as the snow melts, the groundskeeper gives them the okay to do basic drills and such. It's not sanctioned or official, but the varsity team always does it."

My face dropped. Varsity baseball.

Charlie was on the varsity baseball team.

I hadn't done a deep dig in the past week or so, but I definitely knew he was on the team and on my short list. Which guy, I wasn't sure. Part of me was having too much fun to want to find out. But time was running out.

"Let's go watch for a few minutes," Skye said, pulling my arm and dragging me across the field.

"No...no, we shouldn't. We don't want to disturb them," I stammered as fear coursed through my body. I wasn't sure why I was so frightened, but the thought of being close to someone who could be Charlie scared the hell out of me.

But Skye just brushed me off. "Oh, they won't even notice. They're so focused on the game, they forget people are even watching half the time."

I tried to swallow down my fears, but it didn't work. Even though the air was brisk, I started sweating.

Skye hauled me over to the bleachers, taking a seat in the second row, her eyes glued to the field. "So that one over there," she pointed to a guy in the outfield with a backwards red hat on, "is Austin with the fine ass."

I held back a laugh as she continued. "Everyone knows baseball players have the best asses, but Austin's is on another level. Honestly, if there was a best ass superlative for the yearbook, he would win every year. Ask anyone."

I put it on my mental list *not* to ask anyone and let her go on pointing out the rest of the guys.

"Max is by second, taking the grounders. The hottie next to him is Connor. He's the captain."

The one with the C on front of his letterman's jacket. I had seen him multiple times now, but never close enough to talk to. The guys were always together as a group; rarely did I see them alone.

"Owen is out there in the outfield by himself. Typical. The guy always looks like everything is an annoyance to him."

The lightbulb went off. "He's the one that delivered the basket of gifts the other week. Char—I mean, my secret admirer even apologized for him in his letter, saying he wasn't always that bad. I wonder..." I trailed off, not sure exactly what I wondered, but it was probably the same as everyone else.

"Well, he's best friends with Connor. They're always together. And Austin. And Max. Oh hell, all the boys are always together. Do you think Owen is your secret admirer?" Skye's eyes lit up for a second before I shook my head.

"No, he isn't. He actually said so when he delivered the basket," I said, remembering his exact words.

Skye blinked, her mouth agape. "Owen *talked* to you? Owen doesn't talk to many people outside of the guys."

I shrugged. "I mean, I wouldn't say talked. He told me his name when I asked, and then basically said the basket wasn't from him, so 'don't get any ideas.'"

She nodded slowly, turning her attention back to the field. The one she pointed out as Connor had stood up, stretching his arms. It seemed as if he noticed us, and Skye waved.

"Connor is nice. I mean, he throws the *best* parties around too, for any occasion. He's also something of a player and a bad boy, though. He's gotten himself in trouble, but nothing too big. Just stupid teenage boy stuff, usually with Austin."

I heard about Connor's parties. They seemed to happen often. "A player?"

"Yeah, he has a new girl on his side at every party. Not sure I've ever seen him with a girlfriend, more just girls that are friends." Her eyes lit up when she realized what she said. "Oh! No, I don't mean he sleeps around. I don't think. He's not an asshole. Overall, he's a nice guy, but sometimes does stupid stuff. He almost got kicked off the team last year for his stunts, but so far this year he's been more tame. He's probably one of the most popular guys at Ryder right now, between his parties, his hotness, and his behavior."

We were too far from the guys to get a good look at defining features, but from what I could see, Connor was hot. And as soon as he turned to find us looking again, he whipped his head the other direction and shouted to the batter to hit another.

"Austin and Max are the glue to the team, though. Where Connor is the captain, Austin and Max are the official mascots. They are hilarious and everyone loves them. Some of the stuff Max has done is absolutely epic."

She made me dizzy with all the information. Names and descriptions were making my head spin. "Can we go?"

Skye gave me a weird look, but agreed. We jumped off the bleachers and headed back to the path toward her car.

I didn't look back.

Being that close to the guy who potentially was my secret admirer freaked me out. My stomach somersaulted over and over with nerves.

Everything we had was in our letters. *That* was our reality. Knowing he might have been on that field, right in front of me, made it too real. I knew I was running out of time to figure out who he was, but I also didn't want to leave our little bubble. Where we could be free from expectations, from judgments, from other people's opinions, and just be *us*.

I didn't have much time left, and I wanted to savor it as long as I could.

*I*n the past week, I had three letters to consume, all of which were heavy with clues. But Charlie made me work for it. He liked to hide them within the letter, and once again, within a book.

The Sea of Tranquility, as a matter of fact. After I mentioned it in my letter, he said he downloaded it that night and sped-read his way through it. But because he read it on his phone, and not a paperback, he couldn't underline things.

Instead, he gave me the quotes, making me think hard about what he was conveying. Some of the things from *Without Merit* were straightforward, like the part about the driver's license, but nothing from *The Sea of Tranquility* was as easy.

One of my favorite parts of his last letter didn't hold any clues at all. But it held a piece of my heart, because what he took away from my favorite book was also one of the reasons I loved it so much.

I get it, Macks. I really do. That garage held power. Nastya and Josh inside that garage were different than they were anywhere else. Like they could be free there, without judgement, without other people's opinions.

It was a sanctuary for them. A measly old garage, full of sawdust, became a fortress, stopping the outside world from tearing them down for who they were.

They didn't even have to speak. They just co-existed in the same space, their energy matching.

Kind of like our letters, Macks. Our letters are the garage—it's our safe place to be ourselves, to be around each other without anyone else.

I cut that part of his letter out and taped it to the inside cover of my notebook. My hastily scribbled handwriting covered the front and back of numerous pages, each clue bullet-pointed with information.

Narrowing down my list of suspects would have been easier if I knew anything about the boys on the team. I had to do some social media stalking for a few eliminations, which wasn't that easy. Most of the guys didn't reveal much about their personal lives on social; it was more of a bragging game for them. They didn't say a lot about their families or the random things Charlie was telling me in his letters.

My list was down to seven. But part of me didn't want to narrow it any further. If I did, and I guessed correctly, then this relationship with the letters would end. And what if reality wasn't as fun? What if knowing Charlie in person meant he hid this part of himself when we were face to face?

I didn't tell him about being at the baseball field with Skye. And if he had noticed me there, he didn't say anything about it either. The potential that he *wasn't* there that day was slim—my list was at seven, and four of them were on that field that day.

I needed to be honest with him. He had been nothing but in his letters, and deserved the same respect.

Tapping my pen to my lips, I contemplated what to say. The last few letters we swapped had been more fun and upbeat. We were playing with each other, flirting on paper in a way. But this one…I wanted to come clean.

Charlie—

I have to be honest. Though we've been having a lot of fun with our letters, there has still been a point to them. You've been sending clues, and even though I've used them as more of a get to know you than actual clues…there still is a mystery to solve.

I narrowed my list down to seven. Per our agreement, I haven't asked anyone for help. Yet. But considering I don't know any of the seven names personally, I may need some outsider assistance.

So, I think I'm asking for permission? I'll limit it to Skye only. She's a wealth of knowledge on everyone anyway, right? But if you say no, then I won't breathe a word to anyone. I'll do it on my own. Well, just me and you.

I can't believe this month is almost over already. It's flown by faster than I could have imagined. But that means I need to start making some assumptions here. The only good part about having this ... relationship (?) is that I feel like I can take a shot in the dark, and you won't laugh at me for it. I'm coming from no background knowledge of who you are, and every guess I take is just that—a wild guess. I have my reasons as to why I have each guy on this list, but to you, it may be comical.

Anyway. Moving on. I'll see if I can thin the list a little before my next letter. If you want to throw out any major hints before then, I'll take them. I feel like the longer we go, the more people are going to talk. Skye said that the longest someone went without figuring it out was three weeks? Has no one really gone the full month without getting it right?

Because if not ... I may just be the first. Record setter, right here.

Really moving on this time. I can't believe you read The Sea of Tranquility! You're a super-fast reader, almost faster than I am. Well, actually, faster than I am these days. I've been slacking on my reading, mostly because of these letters. When I'm not writing you one, I'm reading yours and pouring over the clues. It's become my nightly routine.

I have a test tomorrow in Spanish and an essay due in English, so I'm headed to get some work done. Send more hints!!!

—McKinnon

Once again, I left out the part about being at the field last week. I didn't know why, but having him acknowledge if he saw me there or not felt like it would ruin things. Like having us both know we were within that proximity of each other, so close yet so far, would pop the bubble. My begging for hints paid off, because his next letter two days later was chock full of them. Some straight forward, like the fact that his favorite dessert is a root beer float, and some vague again, like how random letters were capitalized.

It was all a game to him, and I was always eager to play. Due to a massive amount of homework and the need to spend some quality time with my parents, I couldn't dig into it until bedtime.

After settling under the covers, I grabbed a pen off my nightstand, opened my notebook, and got to work.

First, I wrote out all the letters that were capitalized, ignoring the ones that came at the beginning of a sentence, or a name or something.

After scouring the letter four times to make sure I didn't miss a single one, I was left with nine letters.

H R N W R I B O A

They had to be scrambled, but nothing jumped out at me right away. I stared hard, cocking my head from side to side and biting the end of my pen while lost in thought.

After ten minutes. I threw the pen down in frustration. Just as soon as I did, I remembered what Mom once taught me with word scrambles—put the letters in a circle instead of a straight line. Having it in a circle allowed your brain to make connections you otherwise wouldn't be able to do with it in a line.

One word became clear—brown. Scratching out those letters, it left me with four.

H R I A

Hair? His big hint was *brown hair?*

"Ugghhhhhhh," I groaned, letting my head fall back onto my headboard with a thud. That was not the type of clue I was expecting.

Although…it would eliminate a chunk of guys from my list.

I leapt out of bed and jumped into my desk chair, swiping my finger over the mouse pad of my laptop to bring it to life.

Drawing up the website for my high school, I navigated my way through the menu until I got to athletics. I used the drop down to get to guys baseball. They weren't due to start until next week, but they already posted the varsity roster, as well as the team photo from last year, which had all my suspects in it.

After comparing my names to those in the picture, it left me with three people.

Davis Maguire. Connor Grey. Austin Thomas.

Davis looked like a guy from my Modern History class. And Connor and Austin were the ones Skye pointed out on the field last week.

Connor, the hot party thrower, and Austin, the funny one.

Davis, Connor, or Austin? Which one of these guys was my Charlie?

Chapter 18

I barely got any sleep last night, and it must have showed.

"Up late?" Colby asked as I plopped into the seat next to him. Ever since the day we officially introduced ourselves, we started sitting next to each other. It also helped keep anyone else from bothering me, which people were starting to do.

"My list is getting smaller. Teeny tiny, in fact," I whispered, leaning in to keep the comment private. One thing I learned from this month was that ears were everywhere, and mouths ran fast.

Colby's brows shot up, getting lost under his crazy bedhead hair. Even though it was long enough to require one, I high doubted he owned a brush or a comb. He let it do whatever it wanted, which looked both cute and messy at the same time.

"And time is almost running out," he whispered right back.

"Don't remind me."

Colby shrugged. "Just sayin'. The longest it's taken someone to figure it out so far has been—"

"Three weeks," I interrupted. "I know. But..."

A shriek from the back of the bus stopped me. How could I tell Colby that the three people I had on my list were some of the most popular guys at school? It was hard enough remembering what people said on the first day, how everyone thought it was a joke that I had been picked. If they found out it was one of the guys on my list...no one would believe it. I would become a laughingstock while people assumed the whole thing was a prank.

The other reason I spent the entire night tossing and turning was because *I* was starting to think it was a prank too. Half of me denied it, and I tried to remind myself about Charlie's letters and the truth behind them.

But then again...they were letters. Things that were easily manipulated. Anyone could have written them...or even a group of people. Like the baseball players.

And the name Charlie? And painting? Things no one knew about him? How easily could that have been made up, something no one could confirm?

Needless to say, sleep didn't happen last night, and I doubted it would come again until I figured out who he was.

"Something's bothering you about this whole thing, isn't it?" he asked, giving me a pity smile. He patted my knee before continuing. "Look, I have no idea who your secret admirer is, but if I were you...I would go with my heart. If your heart says figure it out and meet him in person, then do so. If it says hold out ... well, you have that choice."

That's what everyone kept reminding me. Spencer told me almost daily that I was in control and I could do what I wanted with the whole game. Skye made sure to chime in and let me know that it's been done before, and from the moment I accepted the invitation, I was in charge.

None of it did any good now. Sure, at points I wanted to call quits on the entire thing, to pull the plug and go back to my invisible life. One where I wasn't pointed at and gossiped about.

But other times.... I enjoyed it. I loved getting Charlie's letters, and I looked forward to them. However, now that I had names to attach to the letters— real, live human beings that I could picture sitting at a desk and writing—it was different. I started imagining each of them in the situations over the past few weeks, and it made it too real.

And Charlie warned me of that. He said that his rep in person wouldn't be the one he was showing me. He cautioned me, begged me to not compare the two. With my list, I could see why. None of the three boys matched my Charlie.

Yet here I sat, making comparisons.

"What if he's disappointed?"

Colby did a double take, then burst out laughing, getting the attention of a few people around us. "Macks, *he* chose *you*. He can't be disappointed. You, on the other hand ... somehow I think that's what this is all about."

Frowning, I fidgeted with the straps of my backpack. "He's popular. The polar opposite of me."

The blinking from Colby could have signaled the sinking of the Titanic. "Well, okay then. I mean, I wouldn't exactly classify you as 'not popular' anymore, but sure, let's go with it. You say he's popular. What sort of popular?"

The bus pulled into the lot and the rush of students to get off pushed toward the front. Colby and I waited until they were all past before we got up.

I didn't answer him until we reached the lobby. "What sort of popular?" I parroted back. It didn't make any sense—popular meant popular, right?

He popped a wad of gum into his mouth, even though we weren't allowed to chew it in classrooms. "Yeah, I mean, is he party popular, sports popular, the nice-to-everyone popular, or..." He trailed off, as if there were more options.

In my head, popular meant one thing, but according to Colby, there was an entire classification system. "Um...yes? I'm not really sure. Definitely sports popular."

Skye was going to murder me if she found out I told someone I had crucial info like my secret admirer being sports popular. Even though it wouldn't help Colby narrow it down, it was still more info than I gave Skye so far.

Colby reached up and shook his hair out of his face. "Well, who doesn't love a good opposites attract romance storyline?"

I paused, thinking. It was true—now that I had an idea of who Charlie was, we were quite the opposites attract pair. Though, the Charlie in my letters didn't make it seem that way.

But the Charlie, or whoever he was, to everyone else...wasn't like me at all.

"This is making my head hurt. I have to get to my locker, but I'll see you later," I mumbled, waving goodbye to Colby before parting at the intersection.

He waved back, but yelled as I walked away, "You'll figure it out! I have faith in you!"

My cheeks reddened as I ducked my head, allowing my hair to cover me from the eyes of people staring.

I had less than a week to figure out who my secret admirer was, unless I wanted to completely fail the game. I already surpassed the three-week mark, but that was also because I didn't want to figure it out. Had I asked around for help, had I done more digging, I could have done it.

The only thing holding me back was the fact that I enjoyed our letters. And if I figured it out, all of that would stop.

Macks—

Can I call you Macks? I feel like we've gotten close enough now that I can give you a nickname, right? I do like McKinnon, though. It's unique. Like you. Where did it come from? Is it a family name?

Maybe if not Macks, can I call you ... Specs? Because your glasses are cool, and, well, because of this whole game, I seem to have made a spectacle of you. Lol, get it? Alright, it's dumb, I admit. I'm really bad at coming up with nicknames.

I hate to say this, but I'm almost running out of hints. There's just not that many interesting things about me. And ... I feel bad. I know trying to figure this out is probably getting to you, especially since we're so close to the end. I'm sorry if I made it so you couldn't get it.

So here we go. An invitation, instead of a hint.

March 31st. The last day of the game. I formally invite you, McKinnon Gregory, to an epic party. A party in honor of you.

You'll figure it out before then, I know it. And that fact also terrifies me. But, as I've always said, balls in your court.

If you figure out who I am, and want to explore what we can be in real life, then come to the party.

If you figure it out and want nothing to do with me... well, the party will go on. I won't lie, my heart will be a bit broken, but it's your choice. It's always your choice.

This whole month has been about you, McKinnon. I know you think it's been about trying to figure out who I am, but in my mind, it's been about trying to find who <u>*you*</u> *are. Not only have I wanted to get to know you, but look back at the past few weeks.*

Who were you, in relative terms to Ryder High, when all of this started? Who are you now? Where do you stand?

What's changed?

Everything for the better, I can only hope. Because you, McKinnon, have changed me for the better. This month turned out better than I ever believed it could.

In all honesty, I didn't think you were going to accept the initial invitation. It was the most nerve-wracking twenty-four hours of my life. More so than the state championship last year, even though we ended up losing.

I was worried you'd turn it down. What was I going to do then? With who I am, who people think I am, I couldn't approach you. I couldn't just ask you out on a date. I wouldn't be able to get within ten feet of you. If someone found out how much I liked you, rumors would start, and you would retreat.

It's not a bad thing, retreating. I know you would have Skye and some friends surrounding you. But... you just got here. I didn't want to lose you that fast.

But you accepted. That's when the anxiety really kicked in. What if someone told you everything about the game first, and when you realized I didn't want to play by the rules, you backed out? What if you thought writing letters to each other was dumb? What if you thought I was dumb?

I know I've thanked you often in these letters, but you'll never know how they've helped me. Sometimes I feel like the life I'm living isn't mine. That I'm putting on this show for everyone, but no one knows who I am deep down.

Except for you. You may be the only person here at Ryder that knows who I truly am, who I really want to be. But I've spent so long building up this other personality, this other persona of sorts, that I can't back out now. I have to continue to be this person, at least through graduation. Maybe in college I can start over again.

College. Wow. It's not so far away, but the first thing that came to my mind was that I hope you're by my side when I go. Sorry if that's too forward or weird. I think I creeped myself out with that thought.

Anyway. The party. March 31st. My house. Once you figure it out, ask anyone—they all know where I live.

Here's your final hint.

My favorite number? Is six.

See you soon

Charlie

"Skye..." I trailed off, the anxiety building inside of me at the mere thought of what I was about to say.

"Yes, darling?" she replied, fluffing her hair in my locker mirror. She took one glance at me through the mirror and spun on her heel. "McKinnon? What's wrong? You look like you've seen a ghost."

"I think I know who it is."

Her face crumpled. "Who what—oh. Oh! OH!" The squeak in her voice returned, but she clamped a hand over her mouth to stop herself.

It had been days since we last talked about Charlie at all. Not that she knew I called him Charlie, but still. Time was almost up. People were whispering again, thinking I wouldn't figure it out. They didn't re*a*lize that I didn't want to solve it. But with only days left, I had to.

Reality called and wouldn't stop. We lived in the real world, one where the entire student body was waiting for answers. Charlie never pushed for me to make assumptions or guess who he was. He dropped both subtle and easy clues when he could.

And most of the ones from the book made sense now that I pieced it together.

All of those added to his final letter … and the game was over.

"Come on, we're not doing this here. Let's go." Skye grabbed my arm and hauled me down the hallway, my hair flying behind me.

I wasn't sure why, but tears pricked at the corner of my eyes. It was good that the school day was over, because there was no way I was going to cry within sight of anyone right now. I had enough pressure on myself. If I started bawling in the hall, people would attach it to the mystery and start even worse rumors.

I tried to shut them out. For days now, I saw the pointed fingers and the doubtful faces.

But now the time had come. And I needed my friend to confirm my choice.

As soon as Skye folded me into the front seat of her car, she ran around the front and jumped into the driver's side, cranking the engine as fast as she could.

"Not yet," she warned, holding her hand up as she backed out of the spot. "In a minute."

I looked out the window, watching the splotches of bright green grass sprouting up flash next to us as she sped down the main road.

"You're upset," Skye whispered. "Is he a bad guy or something?"

I shook my head, curls escaping from the neck of my parka and flying everywhere. "No. At least, not to me. But the person I know isn't real. He's on paper."

Skye huffed, but didn't answer. Instead, she turned into a parking lot and parked in a spot far away from any other car.

She kept the engine running, so the heat stayed on, but took her foot off the brake and looked me dead in the eyes. "You listen to me, missy. Just because you know him on paper does *not,* I repeat, does *not* mean he's not real. If anything, you probably know more about him than anyone else at Ryder. Just because you think you figured out his real identity does not mean that he isn't the same person in those letters."

I inhaled deeply, putting much needed oxygen into my lungs as well as taking her words down into my soul. She was right. And it was exactly what Charlie said in his earlier letters.

He wanted me to know him for who he was between the lines. Not for who everyone else at Ryder thought he was. His in-person persona was a complete change from who he was with me.

He and I had a relationship of sorts already, and it was based solely on honesty.

"You know I'm right. I can see it written all over your face. So, tell me, who do you think it is and why is it scaring you?"

I looked deep into her blue eyes, the tears in mine threatening to spill at any second. With a large gulp to clear the nerves out of my throat, I answered.

"Connor Grey."

Her face dropped. Just like I figured it would. Skye knew everyone, and everyone knew Skye. She was one of the least likely people to judge others, and I trusted her opinion.

For a while, she didn't say anything. I could tell her brain was working overtime, putting in any information I already told her, comparing it to her version of Connor, and trying to make it all make sense.

Because I did the same thing all last night.

It was my turn to write a letter. Charlie … I mean, Connor … had been fast in his responses lately, leaving me one the day after I returned one.

It might have been because I was close. Maybe it was because the month was almost over and I needed to catch up.

Maybe he was scared. Just like I was.

Skye finally spoke. "Connor is one of *the* most popular guys at Ryder. He's the captain of the baseball team. He was on Homecoming Court every year since freshman year. We have no doubt he'll be both Homecoming King and Prom King next year. But he's not … how do I say this … intimate?" The look on her face made it seem like it was the wrong word, but I understood what she meant.

I hadn't told her a lot about the letters between me and him, but I told her some clues. "The clues add up. Baseball team. Little sister who died. Failed his driver's license test. And, in his last letter, he told me his favorite number was six."

That got Skye's attention again. "He's played with number six on his jersey since he started on varsity last year. Freshman year he was nine."

I wasn't sure how she remembered such details, but it didn't surprise me. She tucked little pieces of information away for rainy days, whipping it out when we least expected.

"That's what drove it home. But Skye...what in the world would Connor Grey want with *me*?"

Skye whipped her head around so fast I worried for her neck. "Don't you *dare* do that," she hissed.

I paled, fearful of the look in her eyes.

"You pulled this stunt the day you got the first letter. You lamented about how you weren't worthy of being chosen. You wondered why someone would choose you, why they would pick you out of all the other available girls. And what have you learned over the past few weeks?"

She waited for an answer, but I wasn't sure I had one. I learned a lot recently, but most of it was about Connor.

"You learned," she continued without waiting for me, "that you *are* worthy of all of this. That Connor chose you for a reason. Hasn't he shown you that over the past three weeks?"

"But...he's *Connor Grey*," I muttered, wrapping my arms around myself.

"And *you're* McKinnon Gregory," Skye challenged.

I didn't want to be that girl. The one who doubted every move she made, the one who put her worth in the hands of other people. And I definitely didn't want to be the person who judged a book by its cover, especially after I promised not to do so.

"McKinnon...you have the choice," Skye said softly, getting my attention back.

"The choice?"

She nodded. "The choice to call it off. To not meet him in person and finish it."

My heart sunk. That's not what I wanted.

Or was it?

Chapter 21

Charlie—

I'm sorry I didn't reply right away. As you can expect, your final hint drove it home for me. I know who you are.

I mean ... I already knew. I knew the person you showed me here, in your letters. And you're right— the two don't match.

I'm nervous. The second I figured it out, I basically shut down. If this was a month ago, everyone would have thought it was a prank. Maybe they still will. It doesn't make sense. There's no way Connor Grey could ever be interested in me, little McKinnon Gregory, the new girl, the weirdo who had been homeschooled her whole life and knew nothing about what it meant to attend public high school.

But... over the past month, you've shown me otherwise. You've taught me it's okay to be myself, and there's someone out there for everyone.

While I figured I'd hide my way through high school and be as invisible as possible, you made that impossible. You turned my life on an axis, threw everything for a loop.

I feel like everyone knows who I am now, thanks to you. And that isn't as bad of a thing as I thought it would be.

Because of this game, I've made more friends. Real friends. I've become closer to Spencer and Colby because of you. Without this, I doubt I would have spoken to them at all. But now, I'm glad they're by my side.

And you.

Because you chose me, I met you. Obviously not in reality. Yet. And, honestly, I've been avoiding being anywhere near you for the past few days.

Looking back, I'd seen you around. Whether with your teammates in the hallway, or even back to the first day when I read your very first letter in private—after starting it with the girls in the cafeteria.

Did you know I was reading it then? In the student union? I took a picture of it on my phone, so it wouldn't be so obvious. I noticed you then, though. You had your letterman's jacket on, the captain's C on the front. I had no idea who you were, or even your name, but I saw you. Did you freak out when you saw me in the stands

outside the baseball field that afternoon I was there
with Skye? You never said anything. But then again,
neither did I. It terrified me to put a face to the letters,
even though at the time I didn't know it was yours.
But you saw me. You watched me. What was going
through your head then?

They say never meet your idols. But what about
meeting the person you've fallen for over letters?
Would meeting you in person ruin everything?

Can we be who we are in our notes, but in person? What if we finally meet face to face and have
nothing to talk about?

What if we have <u>everything</u> to talk about?

I have a choice to make, Charlie. To some, it
would be the easiest choice of their life. To others,
the hardest.

I have two days to figure it out.

Until then
Macks

Dear McKinnon—

You think <u>you're</u> nervous? You know who I am. The
fate of everything this month rests in your hands.

I'm more nervous than the day I tried out for my
first Little League team, the night I had to wait to
see if I made the varsity squad, asking my first girl

out on a date, the time I retook my driver's license test, and state champs all rolled into one.

I hope to see you at the party. I don't want to pressure you, though, so please don't take it the wrong way.

I just want to give you a hug. If that's okay with you. And I want to ask you on a date. A real date, book boyfriend style.

Most of all, I want to talk to you. In person. Face to face. I'm tired of running around corners so you don't see me. Tired of looking away when all I want to do is stare at you, take in how beautiful you are, and dream about being able to put my arm over your shoulder and keep you by my side.

There are lots of girls who will say I did the same with them, but it's not the same. Not at all when it comes to you, Macks. The things I've felt for you over the past month can never compare.

I also have one more gift for you. Open the pouch. If you come to the party, I'd love to see it. If you want to keep it, but not come to the party, that's alright too. It's yours.

Thank you for everything this month, McKinnon.

Yours,
Charlie

*S*kye offered to drive me to the party, but I declined. If she drove, I had no choice but to go. If I drove myself, I had the option to keep rolling down the street without stopping.

Aka, I could chicken out at any time.

But if Charlie—Connor—taught me anything this month, it was to be brave. And to not take things at face value.

Hell, he was throwing a party in my honor. Skye said his parties were legendary, which also kind of freaked me out. I had never been to a high school party before, but saw them in shows and movies. Loud music, red cups, teenagers going crazy.

I purposefully parked a few houses away, turning off the engine and watching the chaos in front of me.

People streamed across his front lawn, shouting greetings to their friends inside. Skye texted me a few minutes ago, letting me know she and Spencer were already inside.

But I couldn't get out of the car.

I glanced to my right, staring at the stack of letters I brought for moral support. The Connor that I knew, the one I fell for, was sitting right there. If I wanted, I could turn around, go home, and stay with my letters.

But where would that get me in life? He was right—I had to be brave. And he helped me become brave over the last month. He pushed me out of my comfort zone and helped me fly.

With one last breath, I pushed open the car door and started toward his house. My hands clenched and un-clenched at my side, my breathing shallow.

As soon as I stepped onto the front lawn, a hush fell over the crowd in a wave. The people still on the grass in front of me stopped, causing those on the porch to turn, and the ones crossing through the front door to pause.

All eyes were on me. I could hear my heart pounding in my ears, the constant thump a reminder of what was happening.

But then...I saw him.

I trained my gaze on the front door, as if willing him to come save me from the prying eyes of everyone around me.

And he did.

Connor Grey, in all his handsome glory, stood in the open front door, staring back at me.

His brown eyes locked onto my blue ones, and sudden-ly, everyone around us vanished. It was just us, Charlie and Macks, and everything was right with the world.

It was also the very first time I looked him in the eyes,

not just getting a quick glance of him from down a hall or across a courtyard.

After a few long, excruciating moments, he finally took a step forward, placing one foot in front of the other with hesitation, as if he were asking me for permission to come to me.

I accepted by reaching my hand under the neckline of my jacket and pulling out a simple necklace. A silver chain with two charms—a deep, dark violet colored star and the number six.

Connor broke into the biggest smile and rushed toward me, wrapping his arms around me and lifting me into the air, my feet dangling under me.

"You came," he whispered into my ear, twirling me around in a huge circle before putting me down.

As soon as my feet hit the ground, his hands slid up, cupping my cheeks as he stared me dead in the eyes again. "Thank you."

I still had one hand wrapped around the necklace, the gift he gave me with his last letter. With my other hand, I reached into my back pocket and pulled out an envelope.

A teal envelope.

My final letter.

"This is for you," I whispered as he bent forward and rested his forehead on mine. The heat from his breath warmed me, cutting through the chill of the crisp night air. Only a few days ago, being this close to him would have freaked me out. But the moment I saw him here in person...all those worries vanished. Though he was surrounded by what seemed to be half of the school, his focus was solely on me. And mine on him.

He took the envelope in one hand, reached for my hand with his other, and dragged me inside. As soon as we crossed the threshold, a shout rang out.

"She came!"

The entire house shook with screams, shrieks, hollers, and cheers. People clapped, boys whooped, but Connor didn't stop. Even as his friends slapped him on the back as we passed, he kept moving, never letting his grip on my hand weaken.

We rushed through the living room, up the stairs, past the line for the bathroom, and down the hallway, finally stopping at a closed door. Connor tucked the envelope under his arm while he dug in the pocket of his jeans, his hand still clutching mine.

Using a key, he unlocked the door and pulled me inside, shutting and locking it again.

"You're here," he breathed, leaning against the door and letting his head fall back with it.

I grinned. All the nerves I had before coming washed away as soon as he touched me. This Connor was the same Connor from my letters. My Charlie.

He didn't try to put on a show in front of his friends. He didn't hide his emotions when he saw me on the lawn.

And now, we were alone, in what looked to be his bedroom. Relief washed over his face, his eyes closed for a beat as he clutched my letter in his hands.

"Are you going to read it?" I asked, pointing to the crumpled envelope.

His gaze ping-ponged from the envelope to me, back and forth a few times before he finally slid his finger under the seal and ripped it open.

But I lied. There was no letter in there.

Instead, there was only a scrap of paper with four words hastily written on it.

It was a spur-of-the-moment decision, right before I left the car, after looking at the bundle of letters on my passenger seat. I borrowed one of his envelopes, ripped a blank part of paper Mom insisted I keep in the glove box, and jotted it down in mere seconds.

I held my breath as he read it, unsure what his reaction was going to be.

But the hard part was over. Even if he hated what I wrote, it wouldn't change the past month. It wouldn't change us.

CONNOR

My entire body shook. Not only from excitement that McKinnon actually came, but from what the words on the paper in my hands said.

It was your garage.

All the breath left my lungs as I read that. It wasn't an instant light bulb, however, and took me a minute to figure out what she meant.

The book. Her favorite book, *The Sea of Tranquility*. Nastya and Josh.

It had nothing to do with my actual garage, or a garage at all. It was the safety of the people, of each other, of them being together. It was the realization that the girl and the boy were destined to be together, even when they didn't know it.

I couldn't look at her. Not yet. Not before this feeling of insane panic went away.

For the entire month, I held my breath. I thought at any given moment she would bail, she would dip out and leave. It would be too much. *I* would be too much.

Especially when she solved the mystery.

But she was here. With this note. Standing in front of me, in my bedroom, at a party I was hosting.

For her.

Parties were my thing. I loved throwing them. They were epic, legendary, and the place to be on a weekend. I never needed a reason to have one, but today, I did.

Dad didn't care either. He took to his bedroom with the door closed, and only came down a few times to make sure things weren't out of control.

And the red cups? Never held alcohol. That was his one steadfast rule. The music could be loud. People could be all over the place, but no drinking.

Somehow, the parties were fun without it, and people didn't care.

"You're here."

It was the only thing I could wrap my brain around.

She was here. And she wore the necklace.

I let the paper and the envelope flutter to the floor, watching as it drifted in the air. Finally lifting my head, I stared at her just as intensely as I did outside.

And then…I reached forward, wrapped my hands around her cheeks again, and pulled her to me, crashing my lips into hers.

I couldn't stop myself.

After a moment, she softened, melting in my hands as I breathed her in, wanting every part of her wrapped around me.

McKinnon Gregory.

Her note was her acceptance. Acceptance of me, of us, of all of this. The garage from the story meant more to me than anyone else would ever understand.

Her and I. The two of us had been forming a relationship of sorts over the past month. Those four words showed she felt the same way about me that I did about her—comfortable, safe, and wanting to be together.

Coming to the party was merely the beginning. It must have taken a few moments of bravery for her to get here. Once she figured out who I was, her entire world probably flipped upside down.

The me that I put in my letters wasn't the me the people outside this door knew.

Inside this room, we were Charlie and Macks.

Outside, I was on Homecoming Court, captain of the baseball team, thrower of the best parties around. And she ... used to be invisible.

But not to me. Never to me.

I finally pulled away, filling my lungs with air and staring at her.

"I'm sorry. I couldn't help myself," I muttered, searching her face to figure out where she stood.

A small smile pulled at her lips. A smile I looked for everyday for the past month, finding her wherever I could, catching a glimpse of her when she didn't know I was around.

"That's okay. I'm not mad."

"But are you ready?" I asked her, reaching for her hand again. It fit perfectly in mine.

Her face fell. "Ready?"

I jerked my head behind me. "For out there. For…reality."

Our month was up. Charlie and Macks existed solely on paper for the past four weeks. Now it was time for Connor and McKinnon to move forward, to explore what could be.

Her eyes glazed over in worry, but I squeezed her hand.

"My garage, Macks. My garage."

It was something only the two of us would know. An inside view of her favorite book, used in terms of our relationship. Which reminded me.

"Hey, McKinnon?" I asked, my hand resting on the doorknob. I needed to ask something before we left the confines of the room.

She looked up at me, her beautiful blue eyes wide with a mixture of fear and curiosity.

"Can I take you on a date?"

Want more McKinnon and Connor?
Grab a bonus scene by visiting
https://www.bit.ly/dearmckinnonbonusscene
and see just how Connor chose McKinnon!

bit.ly/dearmckinnonbonusscene

Did you love *Dear McKinnon?* I'd love to hear!
Drop a review for me on Amazon
and let me know your thoughts!

Keep reading the *Love Notes* series.
Available on Amazon.

ALSO BY
Danielle Keil

Want more bookworm girl and jock boy romances? Grab *Out of the Darkness*, a standalone friends to lovers romance.

He's the All-American boy. She's the quiet, bookworm girl. But things aren't always what they seem. Will their love survive when the summer ends?

The first time I met Brandon he accidently startled me, and the book I was reading flew into the pond.

A few days later, he showed up to my new job with a new copy. Turned out, he was my supervisor.

He wasn't just any hot lifeguard. He became my rock and promised to always protect me.

We spent the entire summer together.

Brandon helped slay the demons of my past while I tried to help him with his.

He stole my heart, and I thought he would keep it safe.

Then the summer ended.

And everything fell apart.

Start reading *Out of the Darkness* today!

ACKNOWLEDGEMENTS

When I say this book *flew* out of me, I mean it. I was stuck in a writing rut, not sure what I wanted to do, scrapping all the projects I had listed, and pretending my laptop didn't exist.

Then, I had an idea. One of many random things I come up with and never act on. But this one I did. Except originally it was completely different from what this ended up being.

So after a week or two of not writing at all... I started Dear McKinnon. Six days and 25,000 words later, it was done. Of course, it went through alpha/beta reads and edits, and things were added, but I've never written something so fast. Or in order, for that matter...

And I've never been so obsessed and so happy with what I wrote from the start. I love this world, these characters, and the story. I hope you did too.

There's a chunk of people I need to thank for even having me get this story off the ground!

Andrea and Shain: you two are my ROD's and you know it. Whether it's encouraging me to keep going when I'm running or telling me it's okay to take a break when I need it, you two are always there for me no matter what.

In life and in authorship. I would be nothing without you two!

Robynne: thank you for loving on everything I write and hyping me up when I need it! I'm so grateful for you and your advice and having you be a friend in the YA world!

Stephanie: I mean... like, everything. From reading my words, encouraging my nonsense, creating everything I have, making my things look pretty, you're the best. The best cover designer, the best formatter, the best pretty-thing-maker, and an amazing friend!

My Dandelions: the best group ever! Thank you for allowing me a safe space to confide my troubles in, and encouraging me when I'm off and running.

Booktok and BookTok friends: you guys are SO awesome! From helping me spread the word about my books, to creating wonderful friendships, I'm so glad I'm a part of the community. It takes a village, and booktok is it.

Readers: Obviously, I would be nothing without you, so THANK YOU. Thank you for being there as I jump around with my books, for sticking around and checking out my work, and loving on my characters as much as I do. I appreciate every page you read, every review you leave, and every word you send back to me.

ABOUT THE
Author

Danielle Keil grew up in the Chicagoland area. A recent transplant, she is enjoying the Mississippi life, especially the pool in her backyard.

Danielle has been happily married for over 10 years, and has two young children, a daughter and a son, who are exact replicas of her and her husband.

Danielle's love language is gifts, her Ennegram is a 9w1, and she loves everything purple.

The way to her heart is through coffee, chocolate and tacos (extra guac).

Want to hang out?
Find her on Facebook, Instagram, and TikTok!

Learn more at
authordaniellekeil.com

Made in the USA
Las Vegas, NV
03 March 2023